DUSTED BY STARS

G.A. MATIASZ

62 Mile Press
584 Castro Street #107 San Francisco, CA 94114
www.62milepress.com

For Kay

and her starfall smile

Do you really want to see what it looks like when two gods go

to war?

—Root, *Person of Interest*

CONTENTS

ONE

"Assholes," I said. "They're gonna fight."

"Then, for the love of the Infinite, I suggest we take our leave!" Xa chirped in my ear. Xa perched on my left shoulder, the cube held secure by a leather safety harness, its exterior shifting from royal blue to dull gray as if trying to hide in the bar's dim interior.

"Not just yet. I want to see how it turns out."

We sat, tucked away, in a tiny booth in the cavernous grubber dive. I took a sip from a bottle of Martian beer, a Red Planet, chasing a shot glass of syrupy Bumbra whiskey. It was my second shot and chaser, and I was trying to make it last. The unfolding confrontation was at the tesseract bar, far enough away that I felt safe. And I was curious.

Two factions of Decadents had escalated a rivalry from nasty maternal insults to obscene gestures and aggressive posturing with their menacing clients and hangers-on. The packed crowd was making space. Minimum-waged waitrons had already scattered while clueless hipster bartenders now rallied behind their bar barricade, desperately waving to reluctant bouncers. A bloated red supergiant star glared down on the scene through the bar's cyquartz canopy, pulsing balefully amid vast, rugged asteroid fields. I nursed my bitter brown ale.

The opulently robed, reptilian Ptoori had a squad of wiry Jaxsi for backup. The sumptuously furred, kangaroo-like Dveshe intimidated with a triad of Reegree which were all tentacles. It looked to be an even match. The gangs reflected two subcultures of the fuck-shit-up Decadent counterculture that revered "the three ultras"—ultra-partying, ultra-violence, and ultraspace. The ruckus produced by their entourages threatened to overpower the bar's background noise, drowning out the ambient shubdub music entirely.

I suspected they were beefing over something trivial—money, a slight to someone's honor, femmes. And I figured they'd continue posturing, maybe punch it out to save face. Not that these guys weren't sketchy enough to pull a blade or disruptor, but weapons were severely regulated. Private weapons were illegal to carry anywhere in public, including in this eclectic drinking establishment called Crossroads on the commercial top level of the Stoli mining platform. The Stoli was a sixty-tiered megastructure on the interior of the Kekk industrial Niven ring orbiting Antares within the Wiley Limit. I preferred a more intimate brewpub, Taffey's, nearer my hangar six levels down on this tier. It had that wildcat prole vibe. But Crossroads served cheap food and had a two-for-one "happy hour" special that fit my grim budget. The free-spending, rock-grubbing miner clientele definitely could get tiresome. Drink coasters bore the saying "Dark Gonna Catch Me Here" in an archaic Englee script.

"Good grief! Must I remind you of your promise, Stacey? You swore you would deliver me, intact, to a Regeneration Cradle." Xa's anxious trill raised an octave. I'd discovered Xa while scanning a debris field for interesting scrap as the detritus—the hapless Shaktla microcube included—spiraled into a stellar black hole. A perfect metal cube, five centimeters to a side, Xa had somehow picked up the annoying habit of peppering its speech with twentieth-century cartoon character catchphrases.

I gestured to halt the cube's protestations. "No worries. I'm a woman of my word. Quit being such a scaredy-c..."

Incandescent energy bolts and the keening roar of disrupters rent the air. I dove under the table as most of the other patrons stampeded for the exits. Subsonics quarreled with hypersonics as plasma sparks and quark embers cascaded around my hideaway. My teeth ached, my skull rattled. Xa and I weren't the only ones under the table. When the smoke cleared and the crackle of coherent radiation subsided, I noticed a silver-gray Int huddled in the booth with us.

"Aye, what's a bar without a brawl," I said in standard Galax as I carefully stood and dusted off my light-blue spacer jumps. I was still in one piece, but I was surprised anyone was idiot enough to discharge an energy weapon. The two feuding armed gangs continued to menace while tending to their dead and wounded. I wrinkled my nose at the smell of burnt alien flesh, then extended a hand. "Name's Stacey Jones."

"Kryz of the Coldara Clan," the Int responded with a six-digit appendage. She was only a head taller than the table, arrayed in free mech livery, her compound eyes swiveling anxiously. "That fracas caused me to spill fourteen drams of liquid bright. So much for enjoying my last payday."

I casually reached over to the next booth, abandoned by its occupants during the fight, to snag a carafe half-full of Kryz's preferred beverage. Then I grabbed two-thirds of a pitcher of delta Aldebaran desert mead from an empty table on the floor. "Here. No need letting these go to waste. Care to join me for a drink?"

"Most gladly." Kryz eased up onto the cushions. A star pendant on her mechanic's uniform winked.

Three ugly, heavily shielded Dyctal station guards and a score of floating enforcer globes separated what remained of the two sides as they bickered over honor and compensation. The bar manager, a tall, no-nonsense Rocosty, demanded payment for the property damage. Behind him, a Stoli justice android trundled, fired up and ready to go in case the offenders resisted handing over their credit wires. Stoli ambos removed corpses and the heavily injured. The bar help cleaned up the smoldering, bleeding mess.

I managed to flag down a scurrying waitron for a couple of clean glasses. I sensed something, looked up, and caught a glimpse of someone on a high balcony, just below the canopy filled with blood-red Antares. An older woman dressed in black, her sharp right eye like a jeweler's loop, examined the bar below. She retreated from view with a subtle hand gesture even as I noticed her.

"It is a shame Crossroads caters to the arrogant and brutish Decadent counterculture," Kryz said. She made soft clicking sounds as she helped herself to a glass of liquid bright with evident relish from the now-brimming carafe.

"Decadents, they were real trouble a decade ago with the Pleiades hyperjump riots." I nodded. I didn't believe in any particular deities, but I did have my superstitions about surviving a firefight. So I offered a libation—one for the devil—before pouring mead from a suddenly full pitcher. I hadn't noticed the waitron top it off and figured it'd be charged to someone else's account. "Now they're just a pain."

"Are you a Gaian?" Kryz asked. "You do not have that mercenary look."

"We're not all Berserkers," I bristled. "I'm an indie buthu jock. A hauler. My ship's the *Skylark*. And I'm from Mars."

Gaian. I didn't much care for Galaxia's name for humans. It had the same meaning around the Milky Way that Berserker had for us humans: a feral warrior breed brandishing all manner of weaponry, wearing camouflage, ammo belts, and trophy clips, and sporting a perpetual bad attitude. I rarely enjoyed the identification, and not because I couldn't live up to the image. Gaians also got shit for being thieves who stole our way to an interstellar empire in alliance with the gangster edge lord Xymry before we could even properly terraform neighboring planets or travel to the stars. Now we were everywhere underfoot. I was a trucker and a pilot with a Teamsters card and a commercial transport license. I favored the tag Terran or Earther, and I tolerated Earthling. But I much preferred being called a Martian and leaving it at that.

At least those names had something to do with my human heritage. We called Kryz's collectivist species Ints behind their backs. For intelligent ants, which also bore no relation to what they called themselves—the Rarjpujpar—or for that matter what they actually were—an oxycarb sysocial species that resembled human mammals except for possessing hollow bones, communal amniotic egg-laying, and triune nervous systems. The polite name used in mixed company was Rarj. Their ubiquitous work pods of mechanics, engineers, contractors, and skilled workers spanned the galaxy.

We both sipped our drinks. The mead had a kick. Boujie bee honey is so sweet, it's bitter. And the yeasts of delta Aldebaran are ever so slightly psychotropic.

"What brings you to this godsforsaken shithole, friend?" Kryz made conversation.

"Careful," Xa whispered, now in my inner ear so my drinking companion wouldn't hear.

I reached reflexively for the beaded cywire bracelet I wore on my left wrist. My treasure map. I didn't need the seed cell of a star whale telling me to be careful with my secrets. The mead was starting to take effect—subtly textured drift and faint movement tracer visuals—so I poured myself more. The bar management dispensed trays of free snacks, and patrons started trickling back into Crossroads.

"Looking for cargo to haul," I said and took another gulp. I hated working, but I hated being strapped even more. "Something to pay my way to the next shithole."

"Do you carry commercial freight?"

"Commercial, noncommercial, consignment, hazardous, interstitial." I counted off the options on my fingers. "You name it, I haul it. I own an S-class buthu flyer. There are few things I won't carry. I don't have a passengers license, but I might take a fare or two. I'm a Jill-of-all-trades sole proprietor. So if you know anyone looking to hire a reliable freight hauler…"

I left out Skylark LLC and my star-crossed partnership with Lola Donovan, now estranged. Kryz didn't need to know about my broken heart.

"You?" I asked. "Where's your work pod?"

"My pod was wiped out." Kryz put down her glass. "By a mining accident a standard week ago. The photon charge was too strong. An asteroid flew apart too fast in too many pieces. My podmates were killed, all eight of them. I survived by sheer happenstance. I was senior overdrive mech on the main mining barge. When pieces of the asteroid demolished the barge, they sheared off the drive pod but left it otherwise intact. I have taken the no-fault recompense payment and received my last paycheck today. Now I am saving my money for a coach flight to our home system, Bakru, for the Reintegration."

"Sorry to hear about your loss," I said. And that's how I met Kryz. I commiserated with her over the loss of her fellow Rarji, sharing appropriated alcohol and free bar food until we were both drunk. As I strolled along one of Stoli's commercial strips back to my ship, I tried to imagine what it was like being a member of a nesting species like the Rarj.

A pod is the way Kryz's species give its individuals a sense and semblance of the mother hive. They don't have a common mind so much as a common hormonal and harmonic system. They create a soothing, centering kind of pheromone fog and vibrational ambiance for each other through olfactory and auditory immersion. A Rarj separated from pod and hive is a wretched creature indeed, though Kryz was feeling no pain when we said good night.

The first thing I did when I got back to *Skylark,* berthed in Stoli's garage, was to open the control bubble where I mobilized redtea, the ship's t-line budgeting tool, to check my dismal credit balance on *Skylark*'s holoface. The two Red Planet beers and Bumbra whiskey shots had cut what now looked like a significant sliver out of the paltry pie chart of my remaining wealth. I popped another Red Planet from the ship's cooler as I reviewed the bad news.

"You'd have enough credit to blow this backwater," Xa chimed in, "if you hadn't bought that quantum gradient back at Denebe FreePort."

"No quantum gradient," I said with a yawn. "No Galasync Navigation. No GalaNav, no way to steer in ultraspace."

I removed the reddish-purple pocket-sized device from my shoulder harness and fitted Xa into one of the ship's emoslings. Then I took another swig of beer.

"I could have navigated *Skylark,*" Xa insisted, now by broadcasting over the ship's speakers. "Here I come to save the day!"

"You'd get super stoned again like you did when I hooked you up at

Camares Point after the first time the gradient failed." I stripped off my boots and jumper. "Remember, that's when you decided to skip down the Orion Arm *through* the Kali Clusters? Remember, so you could feel the space-time distortions? We were a third of the way to Andromeda and you babbling your star whale lingo by the time I turned that slingshot around. Now say good night, Gracie."

I shut off the speakers, finished the bottle, and did a spot check of the control bubble. Not that it needed it. I tarried a bit in the commons, feeling melancholic. I lit a cone of chlawood incense for the niche ancestor shrine that luminesced dimly against one wall. Vapor curled around its golden figurine, a shapeshifting combination of Ọṣun with her Abẹ̀bẹ̀ fan, the blessed Virgin Mary of Charity with her inverted crescent moon, and Lieutenant Alisha Williams with her NASA logo. The statuette was flanked by a chintzy hologram of my father, a clutch of Vastitas cowrie shells, and a brace of glass vials—one containing rusty Martian soil, the other brine-crusted Boreal waters. The little-used shrine's Hellas bamboo exterior walls were nailed milagros-style with badges and medals from my Almiriykh Scouts and moon-racing days. The roof was covered with a sheer white cloth, like a veil.

I ran through a couple of favorite old audios and videos and allowed myself a few blue moments. I'd never had much money, and I liked playing it close to the wire. But this time, it was bad. I wasn't even one billing cycle away from being completely busted, broke, on the brink of mortgaging *Skylark*, or worse, selling my whole operation and finding a job behind a desk or slinging hash. I really needed some cargo. Time to hit the job boards tomorrow.

I clambered into the star loft and snuggled beneath my rag quilt. As I stared drunkenly through the cylicate star roof at the garage's winking lights, slumber claimed me. One thing about those shots and chasers and the alcohol that followed—I slept soundly. No worries about coming up with the next quarter's rent on my berth when it came due in five standard days. Only cockeyed dreams set in my feral Martian childhood. Roaming the kīpuka islands of the Sinai Plains with a crew of tween misfits, partying on everclear in the gingpo forests. Watching a colony of twirlies build and inhabit a collective mud nest under the eaves of our rickety house one spring and yearning for wings to fly like a bird. Climbing the basalt cliffs of the twisting Night Labyrinth before sailing down on a hang glider like a prismed butterfly all the way to the emerald rift lakes of the Mariner valleys…

TWO

I woke with a start, gasping for air. Anxious and bewildered, my head pounding, I stumbled from the star loft down to my tiny closet smart shower where I spent close to half an hour under the full-body needle spray—hot as I could stand it—slowly pulling myself together. I'd risen through blood alcohol and layered dreamscape in the early hours with the ghost of my father haunting my ascent.

Helping Pops shamble from bar to bar in Nyew Phoenix township after a grueling day of construction, then listening to his drunken snores shudder our shotgun shack each night. Getting raped by a Berserker wannabe only to plead with Pops, crying desperately as he beat my rapist to death. Visiting Pops in red-bricked Woolerang Prison overlooking Candor Chasm after twelve hours driving co-op semis across Moon Flats and a five-hour jitney ride only to be told he was on lockdown for punching out a fellow inmate. Feeling exhilaration and pride during my flight academy graduation ceremony finally to find my parolee Pops drunk and passed out in the auditorium bathroom stall.

I kept the lights dim. The long hot shower felt like swimming up from depth, through the heavy surf of my father's drinking and neglect. Like Pops, hangovers never stopped me from indulging. His meager possessions were in storage, but I still owned that shotgun shack on Frida Kahlo Way.

I toweled off, then moisturized my two tattoos. A green, brown, and gold acacia tree ran up my right calf with its roots splayed around my ankle and its umbrella crown nudging my kneecap. And the black-

and-gray tattoo inked on my left shoulder of 'Lish Williams, goddess-mother-founder of Mars. I dressed in clean blue flight jumps and synthed up some shuffrice and eggs for breakfast. And real Bellatrix coffee from my reserve.

Once in the control bubble, I glanced at my FTL ultrawave radio. No messages on the broadband and the narrowband wombly on which I monitored hauler text chats had the usual glib notifications. I removed the beaded bracelet. I then detached *Skylark*'s AI front end to plug in the cywire cable clasp, a hack-free way to access the bracelet's contents. I hit "execute" and the vivid hologram of an ancient star map instantly filled the bubble, a four-dimensional projection of the Milky Way through one full rotation with a resolution so refined the control boards were dusted by stars. The map was a copy of the tantalizing contents of a billion-year-old Kalisthan vodocube, our barred spiral galaxy majestically turning with a particular star and its solar system marked by ultraviolet crosshairs and a feathery alien script.

Eden.

At least that's how the Kalisthani translated, as far as I could determine from consulting the Eta Carina Library AI recommended by Xa regarding what was known about the Kalistha, that third and final imperium of the galaxy's great Progenitor pan-civilization. The library's comparative mythology archives had given the original unpronounceable Kalisthani concept a high correlation with the Biblical belief of the Garden of Eden. I'd found the vodocube scavenging in the crumbled ruins of a solitary airless planetoid in the middle of the Aquila Rift. I'd copied an exact replica of the star map into the braided cywire cable, then strung it with bone beads and Martian coral for camouflage as a charm bracelet. An innocuous bit of grigri. I buried that puzzling alien artifact, the vodocube, in my father's grave in the veterans' cemetery overlooking Lake Koga beneath the tools, china crockery, whiskey bottles, and Utopia conch shells decorating his tombstone.

Puzzling because there wasn't any artificial intelligence anywhere in Galaxia sophisticated enough to trace the motion of all the stars in the Milky Way for 230 million years with anything approaching the map's accuracy. Had there been, I might have begged, borrowed, or stolen the time to run the star map forward four-and-a-quarter rotations to get some semblance of where Eden was today as part of my research. All I had now were probabilities and generalities, and a middle-arm, Sol-type star with six planets, the second one named Eden. There had to be a way to profit from my discovery. But my private search for the Kalisthani Eden, like my drunken promise to return Xa to a Regeneration Cradle to be reassembled into a Shaktla device, would have to wait until I had more personal capital.

I didn't take Xa when I left the ship. I knew what I needed to do, but I wanted to be alone with my worried thoughts. As I exited the airlock, I touched an imperial purple medallion with twelve hooks the size of my hand that I'd surreptitiously buckled to the frame when I'd first berthed.

What I touched was blackware most foul. The hydrogen-breathing alien monstrosity that sold it to me at the Coma Berenices shadow markets called it with a few of clicks, grunts, and squirms that defy translation, so I called it the OxyOrganic scanner. OxO for short. OxO is surveillance ware developed by the galaxy's tiny, secretive hyorganic pan-civilization in its violent, annihilating hatred of the fecund oxyorganic life teaming throughout the Milky Way. The proprietary device detects and analyzes oxyorganic life down to the nanoviron level within a ninety-meter sphere to establish a full security envelope around my ship. As you might expect, the bitch was interfacing the completely alien OxO with *Skylark*'s scan boards to make it work.

To this day, the memory of that renegade hydrahead, who nevertheless was willing to black-market its species' hatred of my kind to me, gives me the willies.

I walked the Stapledon Promenade for long klicks as I brooded about my work prospects. I needed to make some money, and quickly. Antares throbbed bloody above me. The photosphere's mottled savagery with its lopsided convection cells and the chromosphere's wild magnetic gyrations with its jets and plumes barely registered with me in my funk. Sixty light-minutes of infrared granular-molecular solar winds flared from the star's pulsating surface to belt after immense asteroid belt that expanded out to the vastness of interstellar space. The planetoid fields were all limned ruddy by the phantasmagoric shapes and iridescent prisms of dusty plasma gas ejecta. Antares B orbited within the clouds of discharged dust and gas, the gauzy blue-white companion star sparking off cyclonic auroras. Our fretworked Kekk ring hung in this stunning violence, although I'd gotten used to the view.

A dog has four legs, Pops used to say, but only one road to walk.

I eventually wandered into the Stoli Platform help kiosk. The job board was old school; screens and listings you had to scroll through. And Wiley-centric. The listings were sobering. There were lots of career opportunities commanding top dollar and demanding top honors in planetary and stellar engineering—what's called the science and art of celestics. As for pilot and hauler jobs—independent, self-sufficient, self-reliant owner-operators high in pride, low in salary, and middling in skills—not so much.

I found four jobs for buthu carriers, all with pretty borderline pay. One I rejected immediately because it was for a fresh frish haul. Legal or not, I refuse to fill *Skylark*'s holds with those foul maggots and the narcotic excrement they produce. It's a nasty habit, and you can never get rid of the smell. The second was a quasi-apprenticeship with the human/Xymry development corporation Tertium Quid: coveted cooperative status but minimum pay, a three-month full-time commitment, and a junior position. I'm nobody's apprentice. The third listing I took a moment to consider. It was a Mercantile Guild subcontract, low in pay but high in benicreds, for a quota of an overdrive equipment shipment. Maybe if I needed gene therapy or surgery, but I'm twenty-six years Terran—nearly fourteen Martian—

and in good shape, so I passed on that one too. The fourth had been posted that morning. A simple transport job to the worship world of Kapala marked repatriation of a single container, designated Kapalan by provenance but Gaian by location, at about the same pay scale as the Guild job but classified IC. Independent Contractor, meaning I got to keep everything and pay my own taxes.

I hadn't paid taxes in five solar years.

On the books, I barely make enough to keep my buthu license. Off the books, I do a little better, but not enough to pay a fifth of my earnings to the Invisible Hand. I maintain meticulous paperwork and keep my fabrications plausible. I've never had a summons, a lien, or a forfeiture. My record is clean. I submitted my credentials for the job and was surprised to get an interview for an hour later at an all-too-familiar address.

The grubber bar was even more cavernous with nobody in it. Signs of last night's violent altercation were fast disappearing under the systematic work of yoctospiders. The smell of food prep triggered my hunger, but I could wait until I was back on *Skylark* to eat to save some money. The lone bartender wiping down the tesseract bar and listening to fat smacko beats directed me to a turbo lift in the back marked "private." I found myself on the balcony I'd noticed the other evening in front of a nondescript door that slid open when I knocked.

The room was large and dim, suffused with a misty red glow as if it were immersed in the upper atmosphere of the red supergiant star the station circled. Yet the air was cool and smelled faintly of laurel. There was a sound of cascading water from somewhere.

"Born and raised on Mars." An old voice, a gravely human female voice, spoke from the darkness. "Your résumé says you trained at the Barsoom Academy." The words came from a black silhouette seated in the dark. A pair of small yellow eyes flashed at me from what would have been the silhouette's lap.

"Apsis Passage-born," I said. "My buthu level-five flight certificate I got at Barsoom. Finished up at Garobus. I apprenticed at Mandela Spaceport in the Planet Guard before buying my flyer."

"Nice planet Mars," the voice seemed to sigh. A black shape with those yellow eyes jumped gracefully from lap to floor. "Nice to see how everything turned out."

"We seem to be making a go of it," I said. Given how contentious the Tricolor Revolution and the General Commune were with humanity outside of Mars, it was best not to overtly praise my world's socialist commonwealth. Especially to someone whose opinions I knew nothing about.

"I also mean it's nice to see how long-term schemes turned out." She seemed to shrug.

"The native Martian biosphere is fascinating," I said. It was another controversial subject. We screwed up bad in terraforming Mars by not properly vetting the red planet. We'd assumed the world was sterile and hadn't harbored extant indigene life. The consequences had been a disaster for turning Mars into a new Earth. "I might retire there someday if I ever make my nut."

"You carry the standard transport license, insurance, and coverage?"

"Yep." I nodded. "Also the usual Teamsters and pilot's certificates."

"You have any questions about the job?"

"What exactly would I be transporting?" I asked.

"A bit of the cosmic jigsaw puzzle." The silhouette stood and moved forward until I could see the face. She'd once been entirely human. Olive complexion, sharp wizened features, fierce black eye—the one that wasn't femtoed, that is. About a quarter of the face was undisguised slate-blue femtoflesh, the whole of the face framed in silvering hair. A cloud of artificial insects hovered around her head like a halo. "It's an object from old Earth, but not a human antiquity. The legendary sangrael."

"Never heard of it." I shrugged. "Is it a Gaian artifact?"

"Gaian," she said and paused. "How I hate that word. The sangrael is not a human artifact. It's a fragment of the Kapalan worship world. Kapala is an artificial planet manufactured by the long-vanished Progenitors, one of the so-called Twelve Perfected Worlds among the numerous great relics of bygone imperial glories littering the galaxy. By my analysis, it is made of inert unremarkable material."

Those small yellow eyes—close-set and low to the ground— remained in the dark staring at me.

"Is it a cultural, historical, or religious relic?" I asked. I then paraphrased from the Prophylaxis, the overarching quarantine issued by SolPrime, humanity's interplanetary government. "Does it belong to old Earth by ancient endowment or right, or to humanity by birthright? In other words, will I catch shit for transporting it 'cause it's stolen or otherwise in violation?"

"The sangrael is a myth, not a relic." She gave me a weary smile. The halo of artificial insects settled like a mist onto her shoulders. "And you cannot own a myth. How or why the sangrael wound up on old Earth is anybody's guess, but it is a prosaic, nonreactive extraterrestrial object imbued with spiritual meaning by humans when our species cared about such things. The physical object has had numerous temporary individual owners, but it has never been the property of a culture, institution, nation, or international body. There have been examples from old Earth of other privately owned artifacts instilled with supernatural meaning by humans in the past. And many primitive peoples worshipped meteorites as deities before humanity knew better and outgrew such beliefs."

"A 'no deposit, no return' situation if you ask me. So the sangrael's a meteorite?"

"A unique extrasolar object that bears the marks of sentience. For reasons known only to the Progenitors, bits and pieces of Kapala can be found scattered all across Greater Galaxia like a cosmic scavenger hunt. Returning the numerous Progenitor fragments to Kapala is a matter of voluntary repatriation recognized throughout Greater Galaxia and codified in the Galactic Conventions. It has become a significant religious ritual or a cultural practice for the various starfaring sentiences that find themselves in possession of Kapalan artifacts. The process of reuniting such objects with Kapala is also a matter of universal scientific interest. Something does happen when an artifact contacts Kapala—a change in consciousness for the participants extensively studied but little understood. It's a kind of sudden psychological recentering, called 'illumination subite' in the literature."

Why did I sense she wasn't telling me everything? I was fine with that. People who hire jocks like me to do their grunt work rarely want to explain everything. But was I missing something important? I was startled when a dark creature rubbed affectionately against my ankle.

"So, do you want the job?" she asked.

"Who will I be working for?" I was polite as I leaned down to let the animal with the bright eyes and long flexible tail sniff my hand. I really did need the work, but I didn't dare look needy.

"Medea Aeëtes," she said.

"Is there any return bennie in this offer?" I pushed. "You're stranding me hella out in Kapala, a long ways from Stoli…"

"But you don't want to come back here." Medea grinned, her teeth remarkably white.

"Aye, what makes you say that?" I asked. The creature had an interest in my beaded bracelet and was using one of its limbs to bat at it.

"I know a lot of things." Medea winked with her good eye. "Like your nickname, Becky."

"That's a cheap magic show trick," I blurted. I was suspicious and annoyed, but I tried not to let her know she'd rattled me. My given name was Anastacia, but Pops called me Stacey, and affectionately Becky. That's because Moms first wanted me named after Rebecca Wiley, he said, but also from okebekee. I was his little rabbit, and Pops entertained me with stories of Br'er Rabbit, my trickster namesake. There are no rabbits on Mars, although the planet's settlers called the drevgee—a native meta-marsupial—a rabbit. "Now, about that return bennie?"

Mars, 5 Khumba, 2373 CE

Shuyuei Uprising, Tricolor Revolution, Commune al-Mirrīkh

She handed me a set of contract flicks. "What I can do is give you a premium, say twenty percent max on the contract, dependent on job performance of course. That should be enough to get you somewhere you want to go.

"Done," I said. I read the amended contract, NDA, and tax documents before I signed. I reviewed the Floating Island administrative center address and protocols on Kapala for the shipment. I relaxed knowing I could spend down my account to square my hangar fees and dock rental for a clean departure. Then I knelt to offer my hand for the creature to smell before running it over the animal's soft fur. "What is this little beastie, by the way?"

"My cat, Hecate. Kate, for short."

"Cat?" I marveled. "A Terran cat?" I'd never encountered a cat before, or for that matter, a rabbit. Aside from protecting human reliquaries, the Prophylaxis had kept all things organically Terran from taking hold on Mars. Other than humans and select microbes, of course. The cat made a low, surprisingly pleasant rumble in its throat and nudged its head insistently against my hand. I rubbed its chin, then behind its ears. The cat's acoustics got loud.

"Sweet," I said.

THREE

I skipped down the bustling commercial corridor back to *Skylark*, exultant over the new job under my belt. I grinned at a ripped male Berserker strutting in the opposite direction attired in dirty leathers and camos. He snarled back. He was draped in full black cartridge belts and a bandolier clinking grizzly trophies, with a disruptor in one holster and a hypersonic projectile gun in another. He carried an automatic rifle amid an array of knives, swords and axes; a hunting bow and quiver filled with arrows; and an arsenal of exotic weapons to include throwing stars, nunchaku, and whip chains. His cheeks were scarified and streaked with blue war paint. His dreadlocked red hair was laced with blood beads and feathers.

Genuine Berserkers no longer existed. They hadn't existed since starfaring mobs of armed humans spread out across the Wiley Limit some three centuries ago to form the first military orders of knights and assassins that terrorized half the galaxy, eventually devolving into the ceremonial anachronisms and paid mercenaries we know today. No doubt this Gaian mercenary was gainfully employed as a boring, fully-licensed security guard somewhere, attested to by the small metal badge he kept discreetly pinned to his lurid costume. There were strict rules and regulations for all the menacing weaponry he so brazenly displayed, mostly for show. Seeing him didn't bother me. Now I had a paying gig!

"When do we leave?" was Xa's first and only question after I described the deal.

"Tonight," I said and opened a Red Planet to celebrate. But I had a few things to do to make that happen. I opened whitetea, my personal organizer software, which reminded me it was my dead Pops' birthday. My fingers busied over *Skylark*'s boards, first running Medea through the Wiley Enterprise Hub. She was clean—no liens and few complaints—and highly rated. I ran her name through the hauler wombly and got no hits. Then I double-checked with GalaNav on something I half-remembered about Kapala's location. "By twenty-one hundred. She's got to crate the thing up."

"Enough temporospatial for me to kythe any Shaktla connex re Kapala." Xa chattered nonsense as it plugged into the station net. "To infinity and beyond!"

I dialed station information for Kryz's number, then brought up her flickering features on 3D. She was bereaved having lost her pod, and for all I knew, I was her only friend on Stoli. I could use the company, if not the crew. "Got a job out Kapala way," I laughed. "If you crew free, I can take you to Bakru after. It's just a hop, skip, and a jump..."

"Twenty-three point four four light-years," Kryz said in earnest. "When do you depart?"

"Tonight." Medea was keen for me to leave, plus I had no love for Stoli.

"I will be there."

"Give me a tour of Bakru after?"

"I shall do so, gladly."

A job and a crew! I was spinning, a heady mix of relief and excitement. Plus, I had an opportunity to see Bakru, often considered one of the seven wonders of the sentient galaxy. Kryz's home world was a planet-wide, self-regulating biomechanical honeycomb megastructure built down to its core over fifteen millennia. As Xa mumbled away online, I took several deep steadying breaths. I reminded myself of my revised priorities. First, deliver the sangrael to Kapala. Second, drop off Kryz at Bakru. After that, deliver Xa to a Regeneration Cradle. And finally, maybe see if I can find Eden. Then I made a short list of things I needed to do before I left Stoli.

I called the station utilities to arrange for disconnection and final billing before giving notice to the corporate landlord, providing one and all with my Martian SolBank account number for the deposits they were obliged to return. Yet another plus. I walked *Skylark*'s dock, putting away a tool here and a hose there until everything was in order. Finally, I went shopping. Mostly for necessities for the long trip, which included a few cases of Red Planet but also a few luxuries like dark star pastries, Rigelian absinthe, and Gemini tranqs. And a Tennessee whiskey miniature. It took my account dangerously low again, but I needed to celebrate landing the job.

The Tennessee whiskey was to honor my late father, who loved the hooch a little too much. Pops left Earth two and a half centuries after SolPrime's Prophylaxis and a century after the Millennium Fallowing were declared. He and our extended family were driven out of the Free Afrika Symmune on the Carolina Piedmont seacoast when Terran Military Command violently firebombed, force-marched, and brutally removed the last 115 million or so inhabitants of the planet to Mars. Moms was six months pregnant at the time, but Pops and I were the only ones of our clan to survive that Apsis Passage. Now he was dead. I was just four months old when the remaining passengers of Space Liner #144—emaciated, diseased, crazed—disembarked on the Plains of the Sun, so I have no recollection of my Moms. The smell of malted rye triggered my melancholy. I poured out the whiskey as a libation along the landscaped Stanisław Lem Concourse walking back to the hangar.

While I was out, my ship paged me with an atavistic Beyoncé ringtone. Kryz waited patiently by *Skylark* when I returned with supplies in hand, her star brooch blinking, her luggage piled on the dock. She glanced from her luggage to *Skylark*, the skeptical gesture casting aspersions on my modest ship.

Now, your stock buthu flyer stands fifty meters tall, twenty-five wide, and ten thick, with curved edges all around so that it has a soft brick shape. Almost a third of that is ultradrive, and with cargo storage, hardware, and all, there's less than ten percent consigned to crew space. That's a habitat volume roughly twenty by ten by six, one component of which is the control bubble—plenty of living space for one person. Two people, even if the second person is a pint-sized Rarj, and it gets cramped. I'd accumulated a modest amount of personal possessions during my years on *Skylark*, so I grinned when I saw her luggage. "This is gonna be painful," I said, then shrugged. "But we'll sort it."

It was doubly painful because much of Kryz's luggage was stuff from her dead podmates that she wanted to take back to friends, family, and clan on Bakru. I carried my groceries into *Skylark* and returned with an iced pitcher of Martian trimint sweet tea and an unopened beer. As Kryz started sifting through bags and boxes, singing softly to herself as she worked, I raised a finger to indicate a pause as I checked *Skylark*'s page. The OxO had registered suspicious activity at the periphery of its range while I was away, an oxycarb— possibly human—presence that hovered about for nearly twenty minutes. Someone must be casing the flyer.

I briefed Kryz about Medea and mentioned the cargo as we finished going through our personal effects. Over half of Kryz's stuff was stacked on a dock platform alongside a comparable pile of my things, including an antiquated Moog board I never played and a lot of old clothes. We were sweaty, and the pitcher of tea was empty. My employer arrived at the garage with the sangrael a little before eighteen hundred, driving up in a ground van. I introduced Kryz. "We're nearly packed up and ready to fly," I said.

"Where do you want me to unload?" Medea asked. Hecate, the cat, stood and stretched in the shotgun seat. She slid the van's panel door open to reveal a cuboid measuring seventy by fifty-five by one hundred eighty-five centimeters.

I tapped a couple of buttons on my waist pack. A rectangular port opened midway up the ship, and a tensor crane eased out and down to the dock.

"I'll get that," I said as I walked toward where she had parked.

"No need. It's got nul-grav." Medea played the controls so the cuboid floated up. The cat jumped casually out the panel door.

I got a look at the container as she maneuvered it to the crane. The gunmetal-gray box was featureless except for a nickel-colored sigil of broken lines.

"Damn, an nth degree forcebox." I whistled, truly impressed. "We happen to run into a supernova on the way, this baby will still be around."

"That's the idea." Medea grinned, clearly unconcerned with my safety. "Needless to say, it's equipped with a powerpulse beacon tracker and a standalone Escher security system."

I secured the cuboid housing the sangrael to the crane, then had the crane withdraw into the ship where robotics would stow the cargo.

"Can you load our possessions, Kryz?" I asked as the ship's port closed. "I need a word with Medea."

I turned to Medea and walked with her to a more secluded part of the dock as Kryz tried to ignore the capering cat while hefting our meager belongings onto *Skylark*.

"Somebody's been prowling around my flyer," I said as I opened the beer. "I hope it's just coincidence me taking this job at the same time." Medea shrugged, triggering the artificial insects on her shoulders to swarm up.

"I shouldn't worry." The old woman gestured. The insect cloud flew off to wheel around the garage. "You know these hangars are plagued by smash-and-grabs."

"So, nothing to do with the sangrael, aye?"

"Human belief in the Holy Grail myth died out centuries ago."

"The sangrael has no intrinsic value then?" I pushed. The robotic insects returned without incident to settle back on her shoulders.

"It's a mundane, carbon-ferrosilicon composite with trace amounts of heavy and rare-earth metals," she said, dismissively waving her hand heavy with rings. Then she opened both hands palms up so that a hologram floated above them depicting what she was describing. "The sangrael is shaped like a large cup or a medium bowl and was discovered by Alpine Neanderthals some sixty thousand years ago. They worshipped it, dusted it with gold and silver powders, filled it with spring water to reflect the sun and moon, and called it the Milky Way Mirror. The Neanderthals had a better metaphorical grasp of the sangrael's function than the humans, the Cro-Magnons, who slaughtered them and looted the bowl."

"Going back to Neanderthals?" I interrupted. It all sounded like myth and speculation. I'd avoided contemplating why and by whom I might be surveilled, but I wanted to know if someone was watching me looking to jack Medea's shit. "That's a stretch."

"Once in human hands." She ignored me. The hologram faded. "The sangrael made the rounds, almost always an object of worship but one that never remained in one place for very long. It was rumored to have been Lug's drinking mug, Jamshid's cup of prophesy, Yudhishthira's inexhaustible vessel, and Buddha's begging bowl. The legends associated with the object come from various Indo-European traditions —from Celtic, Vedic, and Persian mythologies."

"My ancestors, they had a 'gourd of plenty,' overflowing with rice and drink and such." I stayed on point.

"Exactly. The primitive church interwove all this lore with Christ's Holy Chalice to give rise to the Grail legend that entered early Christianity and featured in various medieval histories and romances to become part of the Western canon. Miraculous powers were attributed to it such as happiness, eternal youth, or cornucopias of plenty. Belief in it attained a brief revival through twentieth-century pseudo-histories and conspiracy thinking before fading out altogether as humanity took to the stars. I picked up the sangrael at a flea market in New Constantinople from a Kurdish smuggler who claimed it was the alms bowl of the Gypsy saint Sara e Kali before she had churches dedicated to her memory during the short-lived Romani Republic."

I wasn't familiar with the history, so I couldn't judge its accuracy. But it seemed to me I was treading a fine line in transporting the sangrael. "So, it's an ordinary Kapalan artifact according to the bill of lading I'll be filing, with extraordinary human historical, religious, and cultural significance no one needs to know about?"

"That's correct." She gave me a tired smile. "But Kapalan artifacts have acquired their own significance. And mythology. Anyone who returns a piece of the worship world is to be granted a heartfelt desire beyond the Subite Effect, a boon according to legend. The sangrael has to be physically delivered to Kapala by a representative of the sentiency that evolved on Earth—in other words, by human beings. I can't make the journey myself. Too old and too many obligations. I've got the bar to run after all. But you're my proxy, my hired agent, which is the same thing as me delivering the sangrael."

Medea seemed sure of what she was talking about, although talk of boons and the Subite Effect was above my pay grade. She parsed things cleanly but not convincingly, and was big on the details but sketchy about the big picture, a combination that made me wary. I wasn't sure that I could take what she said literally, even though I did take her seriously. Again, I sensed Medea wasn't telling me the whole story.

"What's your wish?" No harm in asking, though I didn't expect an answer.

"I want to find the x-star."

Her wish brought me up short. X-star was shorthand for an exotic matter star. That was a legend I'd heard about and a physics I was familiar with.

Dark matter haloes decouple a region of space-time from cosmic expansion through their gravity, catalyzing baryonic galaxies to form and evolve within their non-baryonic structures. Most nested baryonic galaxies, in turn, host coevolving supermassive black holes at their centers and, theoretically, exotic-matter stellar objects somewhere on their peripheries. Theoretically, because nobody had ever encountered an x-star. The physicist Cordain Levsky demonstrated mathematically that a galactic mass is required for the existence of an x-star but that only one x-star can exist in any galactic mass at any given time. Something to do with quantum identity and weirdness—what happens when you take two synchronized fundamental particles, separate them by a couple of parsecs, smack one particle and observe the other particle instantaneously reacting. Finger of the Infinite. So, while x-stars are coming into being here and there all the time, multiple x-stars can never exist in the same galaxy at the same time because essentially, they are all just one x-star. Indistinguishable, indivisible, and likely nonexistent. I was stunned silent by the sheer audacity of her desire.

"Our things are onboard," Kryz said.

"Mind if we load up your van with all the crap we can't take?" I asked Medea, glancing over the remaining junk. "I don't want the removal coming off my deposit."

"Go ahead." She nodded. "One of my staff will dispose of it."

The cat wriggled between boxes, played with an unmatched sock, and teethed on a worn hat as Kryz and I hauled and packed the excess possessions into the vehicle.

"Do we notify you when we drop off the sangrael at Kapala?" I asked as Medea started the van's engine.

"I'll know when you get to Kapala." And she drove away.

"A most peculiar lady," Kryz said, tilting her head to follow the van.

"Got that right." I started back to the ship. Medea was blithe, sanguine, and made me a little nervous. "What say we get organized, then get going?" I surreptitiously pocketed the OxO when we boarded, finding Xa offline and brimming with information.

"And now, here's something we hope you'll really like," Xa's helium light voice babbled. "There are scores of regional temporospatial associations of Kapala with Shaktla. Mostly myth, but a few quasi-historical references. Seven pan-galactic associations, all myths except for a curious entry in the blog of Tarquis the Elder…"

"Xa, meet our new crewmember," I interrupted, opening another beer. "Kryz, this is my companion Xa, who's a few bolts short of an engine. Kryz will be traveling to Kapala with us. After that, we'll be dropping her off at Bakru."

"Oh." Xa seemed startled. "Sufferin' succotash! You were at the bar after the fight broke out."

"Nice to be remembered." Kryz half-smiled.

I divided up the personal space and claimed my comfort place, the star loft. I was on my fourth beer and feeling fine. While Kryz unpacked, I split the three-meter-radius control bubble into facing hemispheres. She had the ultradrive, sublight propulsion, shields, and life support. I had communications, navigation, weaponry, and the helm. Each hemisphere had a full sensor array so each of us would be looking at the same data. I introduced Kryz to greentea, my navigation software, when we sat for the flight. She quickly mastered it.

I filed a general declaration, flight plan, cargo manifest, and bill of lading for Medea's sangrael and the trip to Kapala with the Wiley Authority, then cleared a departure time with Stoli Command and Control. I drank another beer while Kryz and I made one more run-through to make sure everything was green. Then we took off.

Eight hundred klicks out, I took a last look at Stoli, silhouetted against burning Antares in the rearview. I wouldn't be back anytime soon unless a lot of money was involved.

Kryz hit the ultradrive, and the scenery fractaled. The Galasync kicked in as we popped, giving us the galactic LLA navigation sphere. I sighted on Kapala, ran the options through greentea, then keyed in our course with the usual contingencies.

Nine and three-quarters solar days.

FOUR

At that moment, I heard an odd sound, a high plaintive noise. Kate bounded up the stairs into the control bubble with a series of meows, then trilled.

"Where in hell did you come from?" I laughed at our stowaway. The cat approached Kryz cautiously. She tried to ignore the creature. I called Medea's grubber bar back on Stoli.

"Madame Aeëtes, your cat snuck onto *Skylark* when we were getting rid of our stuff. She's just fine, but I don't know how we're gonna ship her back to you."

The reply came a minute or so later.

"Thank you for finding Kate. I was worried about her. I know a Blood Buddhist abbess on Kapala. You can leave the cat with her. *Otia dant vitia.*"

Kate perked up at the sound of Medea's voice. The cat quickly made herself a nest out of my favorite Tharsis fleece. Blacktea, *Skylark*'s operating AI, provided info on the care and feeding of cats, including construction of the all-important litter box and scratching post. In the process, I skimmed the medieval folklore about cats as familiars and guides to wise and cunning folk

I settled into the delivery run for this severely eccentric employer, owner of a mildly exotic cargo—basically indistinguishable from countless past freight hauls. Now, I can pretty much handle *Skylark* on my own. The reason to crew is for the company. Kate provided entertainment but not company. And Kryz wasn't much company, at least at first. She spent the first two days in her tiny cabin, tranquilized to the gills and saturated with artificial Rarj pheromones. I felt bad for her. At least she was eating, so I managed to coax her out of her semi-comatose state on the third day when she raided the commons for a meal. I used a game of Texas hold'em poker as bait.

We played cards for the next seven days. Mostly poker and aklavor. I taught her baccarat and gin rummy. She taught me the basics of Galaxia hidrodal. The card games were a nice way to pass the time. We each synthed up our own meals, and I mostly ersatzed my coffee, supplemented by an occasional grind of gourmet beans from my stock. But I refused to replicate my booze. I preferred my alcohol brewed and bottled by sentient organic beings and recycled the empties into subatomic particles for the replicator. When I wasn't shuffling cards or eating or drinking, I turned the commons into a micro-gym, changing into sweats each morning for a vigorous workout. Apparently, Rarji have a five-thousand-year-old tradition of isometric and stationary martial arts exercises Kryz could perform in her cabin to keep herself fit. I sometimes heard her chanting and praying in her language, performing daily rituals in her tiny compartment with candles and incense to remember her dead podmates. I understood she needed this, even though I'd left the praise houses and shout rings of Nyew Phoenix township long ago. She noticed my ancestor shrine right off but also noted how rarely I used it.

Kate took to sleeping with me in the star loft when I retired drunk for the evening to scroll through the haulage community on wombly under the handle Nadia, read my pulp-fiction Virago downloads, or research the sangrael and Kapalan repatriation. I caught her coolly leaving Kryz's quarters in the mornings. I found a pseudoscientific screed about Kapala and its artifacts online by a Screv elder named Ralza Tabor that laid out some dubious theories. That the artifacts were deliberately seeded along with life's precursors by the Progenitors or were the byproduct of some horrendous industrial accident and were a backdoor to the remnants of the Progenitor Cosmos or part of Kapala's planetary organic intelligence constructed to instigate communion. That Kapala and the Twelve Perfected Worlds were a deactivated galaxy-wide artificial intelligence, an abandoned interstellar neural network intended for cosmic enlightenment or transcendence.

As for the sangrael, it wasn't registered on the joint UNESCO/Blue Shield World Heritage List or SolPrime's Cultural Properties Index nor did it appear on Interpol's database of stolen works of art. But Medea hadn't been exactly truthful when she claimed human belief in the

Holy Grail myth had disappeared centuries before. In the marauding Berserker vanguard that spearheaded humanity's expansion across the Wiley Limit during the Colonial Crusades, there initially had been military orders of knighthood, among them the Blood Order of the Holy Grail. And the Terran exile Society for Creative Anachronism still campaigned for gathering together all surviving human relics— including the fabled Grail—into a monolithic Museum of Humanity on some resurrected Earth. These blips in Medea's spiel gave me pause. Did she have some other agenda for this cargo and its delivery?

I suspected Medea wanted to embrace the sangrael's positives— Kapalan reunification with its benefits—and avoid its negatives—a human cultural artifact designation—which is why she was waffling. Not outright lying but dissembling. I'd covered my ass as far as I could once I determined the sangrael wasn't actually dangerous, but I wasn't prepared to answer questions from people with badges and warrants if it came to that.

Finally, there was keeping *Skylark* shipshape and primed for action. We both seemed equally obsessed with the orderliness and cleanliness that makes long flights in a buthu sardine can bearable. And we kept to routines of regularly double-checking *Skylark*'s systems and instrumentation. I learned a couple of new tricks watching Kryz tune up the ultradrive. And I taught Kryz some of the finer points of the Galasync's ultraspace sextant feature for LLA navigation. In the process, I noticed a series of suspicious preon pings on the sensor arrays that appeared random. They might be a sophisticated tracking sequence from a quantum anomaly detector or a synthetic aperture qadar. Then again, they might be nothing, and I was being paranoid. I asked about the preon pings on wombly but got nothing. So I set blacktea to monitor them to determine if there was a pattern.

That was mostly how I kept from going spycho.

Space psycho, stir crazy, cabin fever: it's what affects planet-evolved creatures in space. And what affects Shaktla cubes when confined to planetary bodies. Even restricting Xa to Stoli Platform had started driving it bats. Case in point, its cartoon character quotes. I hooked the cube up to *Skylark*'s external sensory grid when we spaced and heard nary a peep from it the entire trip. Xa was in bliss, once more in its element.

I did notice, in those cramped confines, that Kryz wore one item of clothing—jewelry if you will— all the time. And she noticed mine.

"This represents the Rarjpujparan myth of the Occulted Star," she said, caressing the blinking pendant. "Some version of the Occulted Star symbol is central to all three hundred sixty of our spiritual practices."

"This belonged to my Pops," I lied about the bracelet charms I touched, reminding myself of Eden. "He made it from his steerage ticket to Mars. Forty acres and a mule."

"Pardon?" Kryz asked.

"The shorthand '40AM' was stamped on all identification and documents issued to those forcibly removed from Earth to involuntarily colonize Mars. Pops was promised land and robotic labor, neither of which he got. Broken promises all around."

"The eight-point star is a symbol of fulfillment," she said with clear pleasure. "First and foremost of the Rarjpujpar Symbiote. Our white dwarf binary star and the seven fully developed planets our sentience inhabits. The Occulted Star also represents Bakru, our communal home world with its four cardinal directions and four intercardinal points. The transformation of our planet into a unitary cosmic totality over fifteen thousand years is the stuff of our epic poetry."

"Sounds a tad religious," I said, trying not to sound judgmental.

"It is that and more. The whole set of elements of the Rarjpujpar Symbiote are meaningfully interrelated in such a way that the essence of each element can only be understood in relation to the others. The star is the sigil for our integrated practice of celestics, what we call the Sacred Science of Engineering. The Rarjpujpar evolved seamlessly from a unitary sentience that covered our home planet to a spacefaring civilization with extensive colonies across our stellar system and ultimately to our starfaring Symbiote colonizing our corner of the galaxy."

"Humanity, we fucked up when we nearly killed off the Earth," I admitted. No use hiding my shame. "The rich and super-rich were already escaping to orbiting space stations, oneills, and bernals well before humanity's survival got critical, and SolPrime advanced Project Concordia around the agenda to terraform Mars and Venus. But Martian terraforming was contaminated from the get-go. Then Venusian terraforming pushed extreme sterilization protocols as a reaction that permanently damaged that world. The other paraterraforming efforts across the solar system and the Wiley Limit— the whole Prospect TerraNova thing and its colonial waves—were flawed or otherwise tainted. Our ancestors, we always managed to come to a new continent, wipe out the natives, plunder its resources, and totally mess up the whole ecology. I'm glad we let Mars go native and we're allowing Earth to rest for a thousand years to let terrestrial life recover on its own, leaving the planet to the primates, cetaceans and corvids without human meddling of any sort."

"We have the advantage of the hive." Kryz then reminded me of the Rarj celestics mantra. "Hive body, hive mind, hive world."

I didn't know how far to dig into the hive sentiment without alluding to her own pod and maybe risk making her sad again. But talking about Martian socialism was talking about the hive by default.

"Our terraforming debacle did let Mars go socialist. We started out with transplanetary corporations in league with interplanetary governments running everything until my parents' generation decided to either communize everything or die under their boot."

I was reluctant to further delve into the differences between the Rarjpujparan's systematic, scientific celestics and humanity's careless, slipshod terraforming. Frankly, I was embarrassed by our slapdash planet-shaping legacy, even though I thoroughly enjoyed growing up on Mars and its unique exobiosphere. I take pride in our communalist successes, with its thoughtful planning and concern for the common good, as opposed to the ruthless profits-über-alles of Gaian corporations and governments.

As Earth died, Mars had been reborn. Reborn being the operative word because the terraforming project known as GreenMars and its fast-track phase named FlashForm went spectacularly awry within three decades of beginning operation.

GreenMars was owned, operated, and financed by the interplanetary corporate conglomerate StarNet and promoted by SolPrime. It had three main components. Warm the red planet with orbiting mirror arrays. Thicken the atmosphere with the release of carbon dioxide from melting the polar ice caps. And infuse Mars with new organics and liquid water as well as ammonia and methane greenhouse gasses. That final stage was to be accomplished by redirecting the orbits of several billion Kuiper belt planetoids and Oort Cloud comets to pummel the planet's surface. In the process, GreenMars was to add sixteen percent to the red planet's total mass, boosting Martian gravity to fifty-five percent of Earth's.

The Ares Survey was almost an afterthought. Sponsored by SolPrime and organized by the UN under Project VitaMarte, its mission was to minutely explore, analyze, survey, and map Mars from pole to pole to definitively answer the question of whether the planet harbored life, now or in the past. A month before the project was to certify that Mars harbored no native life, seven months before FlashForm's assault on Mars, a team of Ares Survey scientists under the leadership of NASA Lieutenant Alisha Williams made a remarkable discovery in the Prometheus Chasm at the South Pole. A cluster of eight stony, nondescript nodules a meter tall, three wide, and nine long that looked to have collected at the bottom of an ice-carved, wind-scoured fissure so twisted and overhung that it was virtually impossible to detect from the surface. The nodules were indeed life: Martian life, albeit of an incredibly complex fractal-encysted type, of completely self-contained metaorganisms that appeared to be the last remnants of the planet's long-extinct biosphere. The nodules seemed to root deep beneath the surface and had fused to the rock over the eons by harsh polar processes. It's not for nothing I have a tattoo of 'Lish Williams on my back.

The Ares Survey scientists never got the chance to examine, dissect, or analyze the nodules. Clause 31 of the StarNet contract with SolPrime stipulated that StarNet abort the FlashForm upon significant evidence of life. But among the UN, SolPrime, the solar corporations, the bridling nations, and the teeming masses of dying Earth, nobody really cared whether the Survey scientists actually found life anywhere on Mars. The die was cast. The rush was on to transform Mars into a second Earth. Into a newer, better, finer Earth that humanity could colonize and profit from. And besides, it was next to impossible to divert the myriad planetoids and cometary bodies rushing to hit the planet.

On May 5, 2109—the Sol date 'Lish Williams and her Ares Survey crew sent a digital data dump of incriminating news leaks, classified media, and uncensored science to the Union of Concerned Scientists, the British Broadcasting Corporation, and the United Nations Office for Outer Space Affairs—they were assassinated by persons or powers unknown. To this day, no one knows for sure who wiped out the Ares team. I was deep into conspiracy theories about the killings for a time when I was fourteen: SolPrime orbital missiles, CIA hit squads, a StarNet nerve agent, that sort of thing. I still have a faded xanthe-denim jacket adorned with "Who murdered 'Lish Williams?" patches somewhere in storage. Six months after the assassination, FlashForm blasted Mars for close to nine months with wave after wave of rocky planetoids and icy comets. The nuclear winter it engendered lasted for more than ten years, obscuring the planet's surface with a Venus-dense cloud cover.

When the clouds parted, wide swaths of the red Martian surface had turned green—green with elaborate native Martian vegetation. Complex multicellular animals roamed in bewildering variety. And the vast northern lowlands roiled with a new ocean, the North Sea, teeming with strange, quickly-evolving life. The planet's sludgy core was re-liquified as an unintended consequence, resurrecting a modest magnetic field and briefly reigniting Martian vulcanism. As the shock over this surprising development wore off, the numerous Terran and solar powers were forced to admit Mars had gone native, that resilient Martian life had fully reclaimed that world, and that short of nuking the planet to sterilize it, Mars was biologically entirely out of their control. SolPrime then formulated the Prophylaxis ostensibly to protect Martian life. But they had little power and no choice over circumstances on Mars, so colonization had to be gradual at first and aseptic. Only when it was obvious that moribund Earth—humanity's original home—was actually and truly dying did SolPrime implement the Millennium Fallowing, allowing the home world to recuperate and forcing the remaining human population to immigrate. Over the objections of StarNet, I might add.

Mars and its alien biosphere thrived under human colonization. In turn, booming agricultural, industrial, service, and technology sectors gave rise to an aggressive labor movement. After decades of agitation, protest, strikes, and insurrection, Martian workers successfully instigated the socialist Tricolor Revolution and established the Commune al-Mirrīkh. At first, this General Commune resulted in Mars being isolated from the rest of the solar system. But SolPrime's *cordon sanitaire* was short-lived as the lost and potential profits were too great and the sentiment "we are all Martians" gained traction.

I was glum my final night of the haul in the star loft, watching the eldritch violence of ultraspace. I'd had four beers, but I was far from sleepy. I'd downloaded blacktea's report on the preon pings that morning. They weren't random, but the degree to which they revealed a pattern wasn't clear. Something might be tracking *Skylark*. Then again, maybe not. This was also the anniversary of Commune al-Mirrīkh's founding when I was two years old, the highlight of my father's life, who often regaled me with tales from the barricades in the early days of the Shuyuei Uprising. He'd also fought in the bloody Daedalus campaign with the Toussaint Louverture Column, something he never talked about. I was alone, an orphan—Pops dead and buried on Mars, Moms absent from my memories, ancestors stranded beyond the Apsis Passage. As I stared through the cylicate star roof, Kate joined me, all stretches and purrs. The strange beast had won me over, and I didn't want to return her to Medea.

Kryz and I spent the final three hours of our flight in the control bubble, seated at our respective stations, running through one system after another. I wasn't sure I'd properly explained Martian history to her as she seemed appalled. Mars was now a truly socialist human society cohabiting with a richly alien environment, and that was a good thing. I did know she was happy to be getting into normal space soon, as was I. Seeing things like stars and planets was not just comforting, it lent perspective to being cooped up in a tiny spaceship. Kryz seemed particularly cheerful as she hummed what sounded to me like soft cricket noises.

When we popped, the fractals of ultraspace solidified into the star-crushed blackness of regular space-time right on cue. A pair of blood-red dwarfs do-si-doed in space tethered to a distant two-Solmass white star. Kapala waxed from shifting two-toned crescents just 400,000 klicks ahead.

"Alert!" Xa squeaked. "Alert!"

FIVE

The cube had said barely five words to me the entire trip, so I was startled by its sudden outburst. A few seconds later, a Gaian military trimaran materialized at three o'clock starboard, not eighty klicks away. Only it wasn't sporting military colors. Simultaneously, I felt the lurch of a tractor field on *Skylark*.

"What the…" Kryz began.

"*Skylark*, prepare to be boarded!" The announcement invaded the comms channels—EM and FTL. The words were Galax, but the voice was human.

The lack of visuals probably indicated I was dealing with mercenary pirates. I should have anticipated something like this and not simply accepted Medea's careless assurances. I'd done my due diligence, but I still felt like a chump. This wasn't going to end well.

The trimaran was a hundred times *Skylark*'s size. No doubt, it had many thousand times our firepower. Nevertheless, I gave it my best shot.

"Permission denied!" I shouted back. "Stand down and identify yourself, or I will open fire."

The human on the Gaian ship chuckled. His visuals snapped on. I was wrong. The muscular brown man with the dark-red braid wore a parafascist Ostara Bruderbund uniform. That meant only one thing: We weren't getting out of this alive. My heart raced.

"You Gaian, girl?" The man tilted his head in amusement.

"Nope," I snarled. "Martian!"

"Honey, get over yourself. You're ours now."

The trimaran started reeling us in. I ripped across my control panels, but nothing responded. I glanced around the bubble, trying to think of a plan. I'd had basic training in repelling pirates and such when I'd served in the Planet Guard, but nothing too detailed about how to cope with being boarded. I'd been lucky so far because criminals don't usually bother with an operation as small as mine. Kate the cat sat next to the stairwell observing the action, watching me intently as I panicked.

"Who are they?" Kryz asked.

"Fucking fascist scum!" I scowled and started flipping on my meager weaponry. "Ostara Bruderbund! Aye, only the most fucking brutal sect of the most fucking bloodthirsty, belligerent species in the entire fucking galaxy. Motherfucking Gaians!"

"Alert!" Xa squawked. "New intruder! Alert!

Another starship popped out of ultraspace 320 klicks behind the Bruderbund trimaran at five o'clock. At that instant, the OxO also buzzed my board from where I'd stored it, to my surprise. *Skylark* jerked again, under the influence of an even more powerful tractor field. I didn't recognize the new ship's configuration, a four-bladed broadhead arrow design a hundred times the size of the trimaran. *Skylark*'s superstructure groaned all around us under the stress of two competing tractor fields.

"Kryz, run that ship's pattern through blacktea, and tell us who we're up against."

"No need," Kryz said. "It's a Conkogi battleship."

"Great! Fucking great!" My sarcasm was evident even to her. If anybody can match humanity's warlike reputation, it's the Conkogin. Human civilization gloried in the whole warrior ethos and the Bruderbund had recently celebrated their species-cleansing of Spica Delta Three. The Conkogin mastered war's technology and strategy while practicing clinically precise speciecides. Rumor had it the Conkogin were allied with Sd†rq*zx⊖ǫrlt•, the feared hydrahead death squads, accounting for the OxO's response to the battleship's appearance. This was jumping from the frying pan into the fire.

Clearly, there was some kind of negotiation going on between the Conkogi and Gaian ships the three of us on *Skylark* weren't privy to. I took little comfort that our cargo would survive, come what may. Hopefully, Medea would honor my contract and pay my estate in full. I had no living relatives, but I did have loans and creditors. Whatever remained after my debts would go to the General Commune.

The battleship dragged us inexorably past the grip of our original captors. A squad of aggro pirate fighters started to detach from the Gaian trimaran when we cleared it by sixty klicks. The Conkogi materialized two antimatter smart mines in the Bruderbund ship's aka-space—behind its shields—and detonated them. The twin explosions shredded the trimaran and its fighters. Our cabin lights flickered, but fortunately, *Skylark*'s shields absorbed the energy waves and repulsed the debris.

Pops used to say when your hand's in the lion's mouth, best to ease it out slowly. But this wasn't the time for lessons from one of his pithy sayings. The Conkogi tractor field was still in effect and pulling us toward the battleship. It was time to act.

"Get down to the ultradrive, and manually amp it up to the red line!" I yelled at Kryz.

She leapt to the task, no questions asked.

"Hold that line, and wait on my word."

A shudder ran through *Skylark*, and all the lights went out. I watched Kryz's pendant flash and weave as she scurried away to carry out my order. I hoped she trusted me. We had no choice. If the Conkogin wanted my cargo, I could make it very hard for them to take it. They didn't need to know about Medea's measures to make the sangrael virtually indestructible.

I opened a comms channel. "Stand down, motherfuckers! I'm taking my ultradrive to meltdown. I detonate at one hundred klicks. What in hell do you want?" I used the rough, unsatisfying Galax approximation for "motherfucker."

Our forward motion halted. A couple of needle starfighters, each a quarter the size of the destroyed trimaran, shaved off from the Conkogi battleship with incredible grace.

"*Skylark*, surrender your cargo, or prepare to be boarded."

The audio was all electronic overtones. The visual was of a hairy mantis, its maw a mass of wreathing tentacles. The Bruderbund I could understand. They were human, and mystical occult fascists to boot. But what in the hell did the Conkogi want with my cargo? Medea hadn't been forthcoming about the sangrael but had been willing to pay for its repatriation to Kapala. It plainly had value, but was it valuable enough to steal?

"I'll blow this boat if you try to board me."

"Simply turn over your cargo, and you will live."

Skylark had stopped cold. The Conkogin probably could sense my engines were on overdrive. Their massive starfighter needles were continuing to make smooth arcs toward us. They were calling my bluff.

I wasn't about to die for a box of junk. So I changed tactics. "The sangrael, you can't operate it," I lied. "My cargo is human-specific."

"We have slave Gaians."

I didn't like the way the Conkogin said that. And I didn't want to be taken a slave.

"No fucking deal."

Xa bleated a warning again. Yet another starship popped from ultraspace smack between us and the Conkogi battleship, as well as the two approaching starfighter needles. The staryacht was perhaps twenty times *Skylark*'s size, with intricate superstructures painted in bright colors. Three ships wanted the sangrael? Medea wasn't paying me enough to deal with this shit. The Conkogi vessels hesitated, no doubt due to line-of-fire issues, and in that pause, the staryacht attacked.

I'd never seen such a weapon before.

A circle of space-time distortion rapidly expanded from the staryacht toward the needle starfighters. The circle passed effortlessly through the Conkogi shields and then sliced into each needle. One of the needles ruptured when something internal exploded, and the other needle veered violently off course. At the same moment, the battleship dropped a half-dozen quark charges on the staryacht. Only the yacht was gone. Some sort of ultraskip drive, no doubt. The staryacht reappeared behind the battleship, released another circle of space-time distortion, vanished, then returned to normal space to shoot out another circle. In all, five circles tore through the Conkogi battleship as it fired back in vain. A series of blasts racked the ship until it listed badly, spewing gas, wreckage, and corpses.

Good riddance! By then, the staryacht had materialized right next to *Skylark*.

I was astounded that a small pleasure craft had managed to demolish a much larger and more powerful warship and in such short order. With that firepower, I prepared for the worst. I was speechless when I saw a familiar face on the comms.

"Relax *Skylark*," Medea rasped. "I've had your back since Antares."

"Thanks, I guess?" Sure, I was glad to see her. But why hadn't she told me she was tailing me? "Mind explaining all that?" I hadn't actually seen the sangrael. Was it another super-weapon or maybe made of stable transactinide metals? Something bothered me, something I couldn't put a finger on.

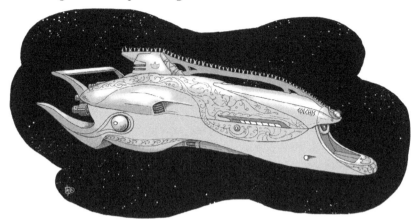

I idled *Skylark* and gave Xa some needed downtime. A passing freight hauler had detected those dogfights. My wombly blew up, so I turned off the ultrawave after a quick 10-7. A bulb dock wrapped its petals around the buthu flyer and gently pulled us next to the staryacht. *Colchis.* I noticed the craft's name as we, the cat included, cycled from one ship to the other through the airlock. The yacht's drawing room resembled Medea's offices above the Crossroads grubber bar—the light a dim misty red, the air cool and scented with laurel, sounds of tumbling water gently pearling. Kryz took a step back as the dark form of our employer loomed toward us. The cat cruised in, nonchalant as ever.

"I appreciate your courage in trying to defend my cargo, foolhardy as that was. And I'm grateful that you took care of my little Hecate on her errant adventure." With that, Medea picked up her cat, tossed the animal lightly on her shoulder, and stroked her. The artificial insect cloud rose to make way for the beast.

That's all the thanks I got. Not even a whisper of an explanation. I was pissed and confused. "Fucking bozos, who were they? And how in hell did you know they were gonna ambush us?"

Medea's smile was not pretty. "I've known for some time that various contending parties were interested in getting hold of the sangrael by any means necessary."

And there it was. "So you used *Skylark* as bait. Better to have them target me so you can watch from a safe distance, then pick them off." I was beyond pissed.

"I needed a way to lure my competitors out into the open. Your transport of the cargo served that purpose admirably. I was able to make short work of those pirates."

No hint of guilt. No word of apology. Medea was a piece of work. But she was still my employer. I realized my anger wouldn't get me anywhere with her, so I took another tack. "How did you manage to wipe space-time with the Conkogin?"

Medea continued petting Kate. The cat nuzzled into her neck as if whispering into her ear. I figured Medea was debating how much to tell me, then realized she was also appraising how I was handling my emotions. The cat purred loudly.

"I did not know how many rivals were after the sangrael. I had planned to see who showed up, pit them against each other, and ideally have them destroy each other. I was confident I could take care of anyone who survived. You weren't in any real danger because they all wanted the sangrael intact."

Arrogant, Machiavellian, sociopathic, or maybe psychopathic—I get those last two confused. Medea had used me as a pawn in her scheme. My employer had casually tossed me into those pitched battles, threatening my ship and my life. Yet I held my tongue. The job wasn't done yet, and I needed to get paid. So I bridled my anger. "How'd you do that?" I asked.

"One of the military goals of modern galactic civilization has been the creation of totally controlled micro-singularities, miniature black holes that not only can be formed and dispersed by design but that can be fused in such a way as to self-destruct within a given time or distance. I have such a weapon and, as you observed, no current military technology can stand against it."

"But how'd you get it," I asked, "when nobody else in the galaxy did?"

Medea eyed me. I sensed she was sizing me up, deciding how far she could trust me with her information.

"What version of the Progenitor Myth does humanity currently favor?" Medea asked.

I was baffled. Fact is, there are ancient ruins, antiquities, wreckage, and artifacts scattered throughout the galaxy. Most sentient, starfaring life attributed them to an origin species billions of years old called the Progenitors. There was little real evidence, however, mostly just legend, myth, and religion. It took me a minute to think.

"Three or four billion years ago," I said, "the first galaxy-wide civilization, called the Progenitors, came into being. They're also called the First Species or the Genesis Species, though they were actually five different species. The Progenitors seeded the whole galaxy with life, built the Perfected Worlds such as Kapala, and archived all knowledge into seven Genesis Keys. Their first empire experienced some kind of civil war before reorganizing into a second, stronger empire. Then their civilization suddenly collapsed for whatever reason. Some remnants of the Progenitors managed to cobble together a weak, decadent survivor civilization known as the Kalisthanite Imperium about a billion years ago, but it was a piss-poor imitation of past grandeur."

Of course, things were more complicated. Humanity joined the greater galactic community through accident and intrigue in 2042. Some 350 years ago, the OverUnity Dominion lost a Genesis Key over Earth. Then salvor Rebecca Wiley found it and subsequently negotiated with Galaxia's ruling powers for a nine hundred light-year "development sphere" that became the Wiley Limit. But our parochial pre-contact origin stories—humanity's religions, mythologies, and whatnot—were entirely overturned or subsumed when they needed to be reconciled with the ur Progenitor Mythos. I guess you could say humanity's was a remix version.

"Neither more nor less accurate than the other accounts I've heard," Medea said with a shrug. She let Kate jump to the floor, where the cat set about grooming herself. The insects settled on Medea's shoulders. "I won't bother with a full and accurate history, but I will make a few corrections to your story. The Progenitors got their start only two billion years ago, they didn't seed the galaxy with life, and they actually lasted for five successive civilizations. The Kalisthani was the last of those civilizations. The second to the last, the Urbunu, represented the Progenitors at their height, and it was the Urbunu who developed the micro-singularity weapon. I found the device in a virtually intact Urbunu warship lost in a vast Sargasso of wrecked worlds along the Far 3 KPC Arm. One of a few tricks I salvaged from the Progenitors."

"That weapon, it was damned aggro all right," I said. I could give fuck all about the Progenitors, but their weapon was something else. "If you'd blasted the Gaians like you did the Conkogin, I can assure you the Ostara Bruderbund would have considered themselves honor-bound to avenge their fallen comrades. You'd need to watch your back from this day forward. Don't know if the Conkogin feel the same way."

"They don't dare attack me again. Not after what I did to their battleship."

"Aye, don't bet on that. They might not see it as a matter of honor. Maybe they don't think it's good for business to let a punk staryacht bring down their frontline battleship and get away with it."

I dropped my warning and backed off. I was still angry at Medea, but she was a big girl. And what did I care if she got popped later on? Still, she didn't deserve to die for being stubborn or obtuse about dealing with her competitors. She gave me a cool stare. "We shall see."

SIX

"Would it be possible to return to my quarters?" Kryz entered the conversation for the first time. "I am tired after that battle. I would like to nap and then to eat something."

"Where are my manners?" Medea said. "You'll be my honored guests while we visit Kapala. Needless to say, you'll dine with me this evening."

She personally led us to a pair of sumptuous compartments on the *Colchis*. My cabin had a full bath, with a Jacuzzi hot tub. The king-sized bed had cotton mattresses, silk sheets, and down comforters. The entertainment center was a surround-sound, 3-D micro-theater wonder loaded with the latest virtual technologies. There was a desk with all sorts of writing devices and a bar with a fine assortment of beverages. Whatever danger or harm Medea might have exposed me to, I was still under contract. I forgave her questionable behavior and took advantage of her hospitality. I grabbed an Ares Lager and ran a hot, hot bath. After a long soak, I dried myself off with two luxurious cotton towels. I moisturized my two tattoos, brushed my teeth, combed my hair, and carefully cleaned the bracelet's bone and coral beads. I noticed that my threadbare spacer jumps and undergarments from piloting *Skylark* were clean and folded on the dresser. My boots had been wiped, buffed, and conditioned.

"Thanks for the hospitality," I said, entering the captain's wardroom. "Never expected to find an Ares in my room."

"I'm still a grubber bartender at heart," Medea said. She sat with Kryz at a well-appointed table and invited me to join her. Kryz raised a glass of liquid bright in my direction with a smile. I pulled up a chair as the ceiling above me irised out, the old school, thirty-six-blade diaphragm opening with dramatic effect. The planet Kapala spun slowly overhead amidst the splendor of the Norma spiral arm.

Think of a world roughly the size of Venus with no killer clouds but a lifesaving magnetic field, with no appreciable water but an atmosphere rich in oxygen. The suede-colored planet hung in the cyglass dome above us looking like a kid's freak yo-yo, two full hemispheres divided by a north/south gap 180 kilometers wide yet connected by a sturdy axle 2,200 kilometers thick, all made of a structured carbon/silicon/iron material laced with various precious metals. Medea's yacht was in a parking orbit, which gave us a panoramic view as our host rang a bell to start the meal. A half-dozen humanoid wire bots raced around the room serving dinner. Quail, roast, fish, boiled and mashed potatoes, various rice dishes, assorted vegetables, and plenty of liquor. None of this feast looked or tasted synthed. There were several Martian grain, vegetable, and game dishes, including a red shuffrice to die for. And there was a separate menu for Kryz. From her response, Medea had hit the mark with this spread.

"This food is bussin'," I said, washing down a bite of savory shuffrice and rosemary quail stuffed with raisins with more beer. "So, what's the plan?"

"Why, we take the sangrael down to the planet tomorrow morning," Medea said. "I collect on its legacy, and you collect on that contract plus the premium I promised for a job well done. There's a little side trip from Floating Island to the installation site, which I'll pay for, plus a little bonus for keeping so cool under fire."

"Oh come on." I grinned at the mention of the money even as I thought: *What else has Medea got up her sleeve?* "Two different warships greet me when I enter this system trying to grab the sangrael, and you think you can just land on Kapala, pretty as you please, and return it?"

"Kapala is a worship world." Medea lit a cigarette, done with her meal. "A world of peace protected by galactic treaties, conventions, and customs as are all the Progenitors' Perfected Worlds. So are its visitors. We are afforded neutrality and sanctuary while in orbit, and we are guaranteed safety and security while visiting the planet."

I had my doubts. Serious ones. "All it'll take is a disrupter and a muscle crew to shred any guarantees and steal the sangrael. Kapala is protected by monks in monasteries, for Infinity's sake, nothing more.

No match for even a modest show of force. And by the time any real police show up, the thieves will be gone, vanished, along with your sangrael." I eyed the dessert cart as it rolled toward the table and had another beer poured.

"My, you have a low regard for organic sentient nature," Medea said. She blew a cloud of smoke up into the cyglass canopy.

I also had a low regard for Medea's veracity. She'd rescued me from the hijackings and firefights she'd instigated, but I'd have to stick with the job to the bitter end to get paid. "One more thing," I said, picking out an eclair and a cup of gelato. "I know how to fire a blaster, but I'm no gunslinger. Packing heat is not part of my job description."

"Nor should it be," Medea said with a tsk-tsk. "I am assuming full responsibility for your safety and the safety of the sangrael in returning it to Kapala."

"Make it interesting." In for a dime, in for a dollar; I thought I might just ask for more money in exchange for the trouble headed my way. I had a cup of espresso with a slug of grappa to top it off. "Ten percent on my contract each time there's a play for the sangrael."

"And if our return of the sangrael is uneventful?"

"Then I'll help you find your x-star. Guild rates, of course."

Kryz had been following the exchange with her usual taciturn curiosity, all the while devouring her exotic fare and downing pints of liquid bright. When we were alone in the yacht's library after the superb dinner, she was frank.

"Is Medea daft? Of course, there will be another attempt on the sangrael. She is not hiring security, and the authorities will not intervene without cause, so there will be more death and destruction. You will earn your additional pay if we manage to survive. But perhaps that too is Medea's intention."

Medea's strategy to use *Skylark* as a decoy to lure out her rivals, the anonymous surveillance and tracking I could never confirm, and the public availability of the flight documents recording my cargo haul to Kapala all meant this sangrael business wasn't over. Not by a long shot.

The next morning, after a fitful night's sleep followed by my usual hot shower and leftovers for breakfast plus plenty of black coffee to ward off another hangover, I did a final check of *Skylark*. I set the still-jittery Xa to researching in depth the dozens of rumored nearby sites for Regeneration Cradles. The bereft, isolated microcube wanted desperately to become whole again, to be a part of some Shaktla device, the kilometers-huge autonomous interstellar machines roaming the galaxy we call star whales and dolphins. I owed it to Xa to honor my promise. At least it no longer spouted inane cartoon catchphrases after we'd spaced.

Then, with the black cat sleeping peacefully on the bridge of the *Colchis*, I accompanied Medea, Kryz, and the sangrael forcebox into the yacht's cramped shuttle with growing trepidation. The first step was to ride the restored Hachidori space transport down to the western hemisphere's Floating Island, an aery latticework of cathedrals, monasteries, temples, shrines, and orders suspended fifteen kilometers above the planet's surface now steeped in night. The eye of the Infinite. This was the administrative center for anyone wishing to avail themselves of the worship world's services, from pilgrimages to tourism. I kept looking out the wraparound windshield, scanning from horizon to zenith, keeping an eye out for any trouble. Attack drones? Hijackers in jetpacks? We were winging our way toward this blue-and-silver structure through weatherless skies when two batwinged pteras dropped down on us from the indigo vault above.

"That's ten percent," Medea said with a smirk from her command seat on the shuttle's tiny bridge.

Those sophisticated aeros might be owned and operated by a half dozen-species, Gaian first on the list, and could either be manned or robotic. I pulled out the shuttle's meager scanner panels and tried to figure out what we were up against. No markings or designations, nothing distinguishing. Our comms were quiet as the grave; no attempt to contact us. The dull bluish-gray pteras continued to plummet toward us. Were they intent on grappling or ramming? I prepared for the worst either way, double-checking my safety harness and grabbing my chair cushion.

"Now girls." Medea smiled. "Pay attention."

We were plummeting instantly as fast as the pteras, just ahead of them and headed straight for Kapala, when Medea expelled two of our four methane fuel cells through the rear vents. The lead ptera caught most of it across the bow, or rather the aero's beak, exploding, ripping skin from frame, wing from fuselage, throwing a chain reaction of destruction into the second ptera, which shredded with more cinematic pyrotechnics. Concussively loud, the threat disintegrated, followed by silence sudden and stunning.

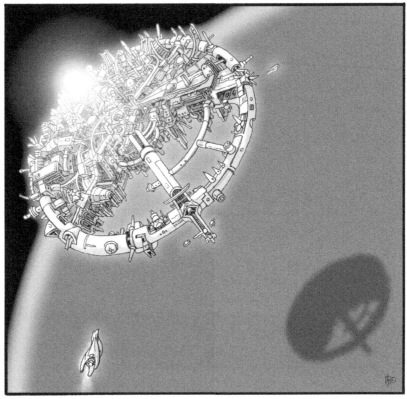

"Brilliant," Kryz said. I started breathing again.

We made it to Floating Island with fuel to spare. And promptly got bogged down in the bureaucratic quicksand of administering peace and worship on Kapala. We were detained for three hours while Medea was interviewed about that little battle yesterday and the incident earlier today. No one had a problem with the sangrael, oh no, because the paper pushers of Floating Island were there to help us in every way possible to reunite this valued piece of space junk with its home-world. But could we do so with a little less loss of life and property?, they wanted to know. During this ordeal, I learned that Medea had some pull in galactic circles way beyond the Limit. I also learned that the two pteras had been piloted by Gaians claiming JohnGalt AnCap corporate affiliation.

"Lots of folks think all Gaians are Berserkers," I repeated the stereotype to Kryz. At Medea's direction, we'd gone to round up some food and drink and three sets of re-humidifier nose plugs with water packs for the ride down to the planet while she secured the sangrael's forcebox for transport. "Fact is, more Gaians are traders than anything else. Traders, entrepreneurs, and travelers. We're a nomadic species who will traffic in just about anything, first and foremost, and only some of us are bloodthirsty mercenaries."

I was being disingenuous actually. The most popular vocation among humans, overwhelmingly, was farmer. Hundreds of billions of farmers were scattered across almost a thousand paraterraformed planets within the Wiley Limit. Next came skilled workers and ordinary laborers in the tens of billions. Of that, a mere 200 million were Martian communards.

"There is the common perception across Galaxia that Gaians are wedded to their weaponry," Kryz said.

"Poor as piss and dumb as fuck." I was defensive. "That's also the prevailing galactic opinion of us."

Unfortunately, there was some truth in what Kryz said. Gunslinger, gunfighter, hired gun, gunman—our language was peppered with such terms. But the notion that humans were all poverty-stricken and backwater wasn't true. Thanks to the Wiley "development sphere" and Xymry patronage, humans occupied some of the highest positions of galactic power and were among the richest individuals in Galaxia. Despite Gaian corporate wealth dominating such institutions as the Intergalactic Monetary Fund, we were forever branded as Berserkers for the marauding terrorist phase of our history.

"I have never considered you a typical Gaian," Kryz acknowledged. We walked along satiglass arcades and rode satiglass lifts to the post exchange on Medea's errand.

"I'm a freelancer," I said. "Meaning I'm not a member of any corporation or clan. *Skylark* is equipped with standard armaments, but I've never owned a gun in my life."

I fiercely identify as Martian. Mars may no longer be the red planet literally, but it remained a revolutionary socialist commonwealth of cooperatives and communes, unions and syndicates, collectives and councils. Our native biosphere flourished thanks to the Prophylaxis, and Mars profitably raised and exported "exotic" plants and animals to the rest of humanity and the galaxy. I'd helped bring in the harvests —amber pastures of shuffrice and fields of blue-vined gribbia tubers on the Tharsis Plateau—first while in the Scouts and then the Red Youth Brigades. Then it was maintaining the fish ponds and mollusk ladders of the Octavia Butler Aquatic Preserve in the Nirgal Valley during spawning season. Thanks to our planet's communalist claims on the remaining millions of asteroids in the Main Belt, our Lagrange foundries and factories had become the industrial hub of the solar system. When I needed to upgrade *Skylark*'s cargo capacity, I could find none better to do the job than the L5 Vulcan Works Soviet, financed of course through the People's Bank.

Funny me being such a booster of Martian socialism when I was in such an individualistic occupation. I had my Interstellar Solidarity of Teamsters union card, but I also had my pride and independence. In short, I didn't work well with others. Truckers, freight haulers, and pilots like me, it's like corralling dark energy or lassoing the solar wind to get us to cooperate. I'd learned in grade school that during the brief communizing experiments in twentieth-century Spain, revolutionary anarchists allowed family businesses and individual entrepreneurs—anyone who didn't use wage labor—to operate in the collectivized economy.

The Millennium Fallowing forced refugees from the Caribbean, the Amazon, and the coastal plains of North America to migrate from Earth to form an indentured polyglot society on Mars in what has been called the Last Enclosure Movement. We spoke a mongrel patois, but Martian society hadn't yet overcome its insularity and small-mindedness over the last six generations to fuse into a vibrant cooperative community. I left the confines of that "small planet" parochialism after I became a certified star pilot traveling the galaxy. Pops never escaped it. A hero of the Tricolor Revolution, he hadn't managed to capitalize on Commune al-Mirrīkh's victory to achieve personal stability and respectability, let alone success. He died angry and bitter, a falling-down drunk convicted of manslaughter. On good days, Pops told me we were proud of our Gullah identity, Geechee heritage, and African ancestry. On bad days, he said the white power structure would never treat us as equals. I honored his memory by living by his favorite saying: If you don't know where you're going, at least know where you come from.

We took arched satiglass cloisters to Floating Island's monastic mall, which housed the commissary, refectories, and PX where we could shop for supplies. According to regulations, we had to exchange the shuttle for a slider, and that meant breathing the atmosphere of Kapala, which was sterilized and scrubbed of virtually any water vapor by processes as yet not fully understood. Prolonged exposure dried out the mouth, throat, and lungs, irritating them and triggering wheezing, coughing, shortness of breath, and nosebleeds. The air on Floating Island was suitably humidified.

The suns rose as we walked through the PX, then the commissary. I got myself a half-liter bottle of Olympus Mons ale, strictly for personal hydration, along with our other comestibles, water, and re-humidifier equipment. The two suns were hotter and brighter through the satiglass than I expected, glinting off the surrounding eclectic temple architectures. Kapala orbits a pair of red dwarfs—K and M, respectively—one of the most boring things for a planet to circle because red dwarfs live for a hell of a long time cosmologically speaking and because binary star systems are quite stable most of the time. In turn, the Kapala system orbits a distant Main Sequence A0 star that, push comes to shove, could easily be abandoned. The whole arrangement is Progenitor celestics, engineered from the fabricated planet to the stellar placement. Who knows what the Progenitors used Kapala for. Not for worship, that's for sure. The place was harsh.

We exited from the lift onto the garage level where Medea had parked the shuttle, carrying our supplies and groceries. We heard Medea's voice echoing from somewhere nearby. I was about to call out that we'd returned when I caught the hiss and click of a response.

"You're making a mistake trying to take the sangrael," we heard Medea say. Loud.

"Our only mistake shall be to allow the witch to live," was the reply in stilted Galax.

Kryz and I eased around a couple of spacecraft and a carbo-concrete pylon to see our employer, Medea, standing all in black near the sangrael forcebox. The nul-grav forcebox rested lightly on the garage floor between our shuttle and a flimsy slider by the open garage door. Medea stood next to the slider facing us, but she also faced an exo-armored, arthropod-like creature, a Glinkku, brandishing a pelu axe in one claw and a blaster in another. It also had two free claws with which to threaten mayhem. Medea's insects swarmed above her in agitated murmuration, waiting for her signal to attack. And I detected something stirring to the left, behind a sleek starlane roadster. Considering what I knew about Medea, I was sorry for the Glinkku.

"You'll never crack all the failsafes," she said.

"Let us worry about that." The Glinkku suddenly whipped the shiny axe at Medea.

But she wasn't there anymore. Instead, she crouched in front of the forcebox, a light-dagger in hand, the axe clattering away uselessly further into the garage. Her robotic insects mobbed the creature, only to bounce loudly but harmlessly off its exoskeleton. Medea parried, the Glinkku feinted, and she sheared off three of its six appendages.

Somehow it remained standing to fight with its three remaining appendages. It aimed the blaster for Medea but hit the forcebox without consequence because again she wasn't there. As she finished off the Glinkku near the slider, cutting it in half down the midsection, a second fully-armed Glinkku stepped out from behind the roadster. It aimed at the unsuspecting Medea as I heaved the Olympus Mons. The bottle seemed to take an impossibly long time to arc through the air before exploding in glass and beer against the second startled Glinkku, causing it to misfire and allowing Medea to eviscerate it too.

That was the second attempt. Third if the space battles were counted. Pops liked to say "third time's a charm," so maybe we were now free and clear.

SEVEN

"No damage to this baby," she said as she walked around the unscuffed, unsinged forcebox. The sigil floated gray on gray.

"I was looking forward to drinking that beer." I laughed.

"That's some pitching arm," Medea said.

"I skipped stones on Lake Oudemans," I said. "And played fall ball when I was a kid on Mars. I was also captain of my Little League team."

"I'm pleased we came through that unscathed."

"My paycheck, it's looking fatter and fatter." I grinned, and Medea arched an eyebrow.

"We'll settle up come payday," Medea reassured me.

"Aye, but 'witch'?" I asked. "Sounds like it's getting personal."

"Hard words break no bones." Her tone was dismissive.

"I had never heard of the sangrael before this flight." Kryz was flabbergasted. "Or of any Kapalan artifacts for that matter. The Rarjpujparan were never cursed with such an object. I knew this sangrael was our cargo, but I had no notion of its significance. It must be valuable for so many dubious individuals to want it."

"With us humans, I get it," I said to Medea. "You said the sangrael was around for most of our history and prehistory. But you've never said why aliens would want it. I thought you said the sangrael is unremarkable and inert? What's got the Glinkku, or for that matter the Conkogi, so hot on snatching it?"

Man, I do not enjoy the smell of disemboweled alien. Standing and waiting around, I really missed that beer. Floating Island security, such as it was, came down to investigate the discharge of high-energy weapons in our confined space. A High Cassiopeian priestess wound up giving Medea a mini-lecture about playing better with others and staying out of trouble and other such platitudes while Kryz and I cleaned up the remains. She got her landing papers stamped as the local authorities were all too happy to see us complete our delivery of the sangrael.

"It is inert." Medea returned to my questions. We loaded and lashed the forcebox onto the slider. Then we buckled our safety harnesses in the slider's flimsy cockpit, filled its humidifier tanks, and inserted our nasal re-humidifiers. "It has no intrinsic value or unusual composition or useful function. Until it is brought into contact with Kapala, that is, at which time there is a marked reaction that can be measured and exploited by the possessor, apparently to gain knowledge directed by inquiry. The sangrael is one of thousands of pieces from this planet scattered across the galaxy. Perhaps millions. So what if this chunk of Kapala called the sangrael has a particular cultural resonance with humans and may even motivate some of our species into rash behavior hoping to acquire it? Or that other species might consider there is power in the pieces themselves or in returning them to Kapala, with or without any affiliation to them? It's a distraction, nothing more."

"I've researched some of the legends surrounding the sangrael," I said. I had no reason to doubt Medea's word. She'd appropriated an awesome alien super-weapon, so maybe she wasn't talking out her ass about the sangrael not being a significant sacred object. Still, something didn't sound quite true. "The Holy Grail inspiring Byzantium, medieval knights, King Arthur, the Fisher King, all that fairytale crap. I'm more interested in why this object is so sought after. Why are sentiences willing to steal it, kill for it, die for it? Would they wish to buy it instead, and for how much? And what's so special about Kapalan artifacts generally? What happens during the Subite Effect when a piece of Kapala gets returned? What purpose did the Progenitors have in scattering them and then having them returned?"

"We're about to find out."

She started up the slider and revved it to a high whine. Then she eased it out of Floating Island's garage and into the open air. The slider, as its name indicated, was not designed for flight, so it fell slowly to the planet's surface. That's when all three of us expected another attempt to steal the sangrael. But nothing untoward happened on the descent. We touched down a little after two and set the slider driving on a course for the closest edge of the great gap. Given the slider's maximum speed, that meant that we had a sixteen-hour ride through the most desolate wasteland imaginable. Nothing but flat rocky plain in every direction, curved at the horizon, beneath a sheer cloudless sky growing ever darker. Talk about being exposed, like bugs crawling across this stone world.

"Kapala does not support life," Medea said, contemplating the setting suns toward which we drove. "Not even microbial life. Which is odd given the number and variety of visitors that the planet experiences. The complete lack of water has something to do with it, but it's almost as if something in the design and construction of Kapala inhibits the formation and maintenance of organic life."

Medea rattled on about Kapala's unique features—the lack of climate and erosion, no apparent geological activity, still-mysterious processes that healed even meteoroid blemishes—while I grew increasingly uneasy. I feared another attack and wanted a beer. We were sitting ducks beneath a deepening star-drenched night. Kapala's angle on the Milky Way was profuse, providing us the equivalent of a dim moonlight that the slider's basic instrumentation augmented. The luxuriant starscape reminded me of nighttime skies on Mars when I was a kid. By this light, I could tell Kryz was jumpy too.

I wasn't buying Medea's explanations of the sangrael or her cavalier response to the violent attempts to take it away from us. I kept looking around, scanning the sky, checking the horizon for lights in the distance. I imagined space lasers, maybe outlaw cyborg bikers. But despite my commitment to keep alert against danger, I fell asleep as we lumbered along, Kryz's star brooch pulsing hypnotically in my dreams. When I woke—my eyes gritty and dry—the faintest flickerings of dawn followed the slider. I wasn't happy about being stone sober. Kryz chuckled in her sleep while Medea peered ahead toward a line of scaly Quonset huts that rose rudely from the gray ground. The blackness of the gap between Kapala's two planetary hemispheres loomed beyond. According to Kapala's authorities, taking a slow slider ride from the Floating Island landing point to the gap was intended to be meditative. Part of the worship experience. I was agitated, not at all peaceful or of a mind to be worshipful. By the looks of it, neither were Medea or Kryz.

The robotics at the cliffside station parked our slider when we arrived, then helped us load the forcebox into a spidery wallcrawler. A dented 'droid patrolled the parking lot full of sliders cleaning up trash.

Compared to the Progenitor's planetary mega-architecture all around us, Galaxia's technology looked small and shoddy. Once Medea keyed in the sangrael's particulars, Floating Island's AI spit out our destination, an escarpment cubby fifteen klicks horizontal and fifty-two klicks vertical, down into Kapala's abyss. First one, then the other sun rose. The wallcrawler powered up, we strapped ourselves in, and the ensemble moved crablike down the sheer wall at a fair clip. There were enough worshipping species who didn't appreciate getting to their pews via the mega precipice that this leg of the pilgrimage was handled with alacrity.

I was suddenly aware that a warbird paralleled our progress, hanging across from us in the gap. I vaguely remember that the vessel had risen silently from the depths when a brilliant beam of light pinned us to the cliff wall. A voice, human without a doubt, boomed into the vast chasm.

"Halt! Prepare to surrender Medea or you will be boarded."

I was strapped in, unable to move. I could no longer see the warbird because the searchlight was so bright. But I could see Medea. She was stolid. The artificial insects had taken flight into their cloud, but the cloud was taking on a purposeful movement around her head. She stared with determination into the light, and the insects spiraled out toward the warbird a half-klick off, their reach extending along the light beam as the spiral's radius tightened. At the same time, the spotlight seemed to grow more intense, as if the warbird approached. I quelled my urge to unstrap and escape. There was none.

Medea gestured, a sign so quick that I didn't catch its complexity. The arc light went out with a loud pop. An orange explosion spread across the prow of the warbird in a cracking pattern. The eruption blossomed and branched until the whole vessel was veined with flame. That's when I recognized the model: Janissary Roc from the Sirius Social Republic. Yet another fringe Terran sect. But they hadn't demanded the sangrael!

The warbird was already losing altitude. It started to spin when the whole fuselage was engulfed. It fell for a long time, burning, spinning, belching smoke and rocket fumes before finally exploding hundreds of klicks deeper. After the blast came thunder, then silence.

"Time to unload the forcebox" was all Medea said as she touched the box's sigil. She was so blasé about the attack I double-checked we were all in one piece. I needed to be sure we were actually safe.

She had never halted the wallcrawler, so we were stopped over our destination. I helped Medea maneuver the sangrael's forcebox into a worship cubby, a precision-carved cubicle cave in the cliffside. The space itself was empty, the light ambient blue, the air still, the stone smooth.

We were in the middle of unlocking the forcebox when a whirligig hovered at the entrance. I knew we were in for a visit from the planetary authorities, laughable as they were. A pair of robed Chabro peace monks stepped down into the cave and proceeded to take turns dressing us down, lecturing us ineffectually. How we had needlessly endangered lives. How we had actually destroyed property and killed sentiency. How we had violated every Kapalan rule and regulation and would be subject to heavy fines and stringent punishments. Their remonstrations were actually directed toward Medea as we were merely the hired help. She remained impassive. I kept a straight face, fearing they might punish her more harshly if the help started laughing. They gave her a digital citation, then left us in a huff.

I depolarized the forcebox with a compression thump. Kryz cracked the box's vacuum with a sibilant whoosh. And Medea lifted the sangrael from the dense carbon foam cushioning with a satisfied grin.

"It is not the object which is special." Kryz stared up at Medea. "It is the possessor who is special. It is you who they are after. They chase the sangrael only because you have it. The Gaians are after you, and the other species are chasing the Gaians. You are the center of this storm."

The sangrael shifted from gold to amber and then to ruby as Medea turned it in her hands. Otherwise, it was an unassuming object that resembled utilitarian kitchen tableware. Medea at first ignored Kryz's comment.

"On old Earth before the Fallowing," Medea said, "humans hunted magnificent beasts called rhinoceros whose horns were hacked off from their abandoned corpses and ground to fine powder for fake medicines and aphrodisiacs. Rhinoceros horn has no such properties, but that didn't stop people from driving the animals into extinction on that belief. Some believe that remnants of this worship world hold some magical or mystical power, or that reuniting them with Kapala confers special powers beyond the Subite Effect. I'd like to believe there's a reward for repatriating the sangrael, but I think those ideas are mostly false. Beliefs, even false ones, can hold power."

"Aye, so you said you would get the credit for returning the sangrael to Kapala," I reminded her. "The boon you mentioned. You're listed as the owner of the sangrael on *Skylark*'s cargo manifest and flight documents. Everyone knew what I was transporting and who I was transporting it for. We're all three implicated in this repatriation and, according to legend, we share equally in the boon. I doubt the Kapalan authorities ever handled five separate violent attempts to intercept a single worship world fragment before."

"That might be," Medea acknowledged. "Myth may be stronger than fact when it comes to the sangrael, its repatriation, and my reputation. Such objects have been the focus of a defining mythos or a cultural treasure or a hero's quest for numerous species. Their repatriation has been fraught with mystery and conjecture. And I have my enemies, human foes more ancient than the Sirius Republic or the Ostara Bruderbund. I was on the winning side of a primordial war in heaven, a theomachy whose vanquished pursue me to this day. So take your pick; implacable foes, traditional cultural beliefs, or unfounded mystical claims."

The forcebox was deactivated but still nul-grav, so I easily shunted the empty container to the back wall. Kryz whisked away the remaining debris from the battle with the warbird. And Medea positioned herself in the center of our cubicle. Two-tone ruby light from the suns crept down Kapala's slot on the other side of the planet, so the cubicle's cool ambient blue warmed.

"The moment of truth," I said, trying to keep the skepticism out of my voice. I wanted evidence this was a mystical object, but I suspected it would be a dud. I also liked to think Eden was real and that I'd discovered the Kalisthani map there, which I carried in my bracelet. But it wasn't like I was prepping for the trip or even telling people about it.

"I understand it helps to keep a question or inquiry in mind during the experience," Medea advised.

She knelt and placed the sangrael on the floor. There was an audible, then a visceral click. As Medea stood, the cubicle's walls seemed to evaporate, leaving the three of us arranged on an ever-expanding field of coruscated light. I grew aware of my companions, the details in their faces sharpening, the significance of their gestures deepening. I felt lightheaded, a little intoxicated, and safe. My body tingled, the bracelet on my wrist vibrated. It was an extraordinarily pleasant sensation. A part of me detached and floated above the tableau, removed from any drama about to unfold, even as I remained in my body experiencing what was happening through my senses, anticipating whatever might occur with growing excitement.

A separate reality shimmered hot behind this world, apprehended by a clear sight beyond ordinary vision and comprehended by a deep gnosis transcending mundane knowledge. I witnessed òrìsàs become saints, and demiurges become gods. Warrior Oya took my left hand to turn into Saint Brigit. Mother Kālī took my right hand to change into Mother Mary. I was burning electromagnetism. I was warping space-time. I was quantum singularity. I was holy, all was holy, all was one.

World without end.

My mind and body were interleaved, blessed, and still. I contemplated my star map and the promise it revealed once again. A nightmare of the past, like a snuff movie playing in an abandoned cinema, scrolled through my senses, filling me with terrible awe.

In the beginning was violence. The primal violence of a universe—of all space-time—erupting from a singularity, of an infinitesimal blackbody kernel detonating into cosmic existence, of grinding darkness layering up into infinite light. The violence of Medea witnessing her two sons murdered by an ancient Corinthian mob, ripped limb from limb, heads paraded on pikes. The violence of my rape, watching my father murder my rapist with his fists, huddled crying between my dead rapist and exhausted Pops. The violence of Kryz's podmates annihilated by an industrial accident, the rending of metal and stone, flesh and bone, feeling their lives instantly extinguished. Violence and trauma laid bare for the three of us to see. The violence of birth and death become identity. Each of us was a starting point defined by our violence.

The cubicle, the three of us, and the sangrael all appeared to simultaneously melt and congeal, undulate and glaze over, pockmark and fill in, fragment and unify, agitate and calm down. There were beauty and horror, reason and madness, joy and terror in each moment. Demons and angels wrestled within me. The detached me noticed three vanishing points forming, one located behind each of us. The vanishing points became nodes of light, then blossomed into stars as convergence lines radiated out through the three of us, each of us a starting point now intersecting as our opaque bodies became translucent, then transparent. All that was left of me was the beaded cywire bracelet through which the lines of my destiny merged. Birth was violence, with a chance for rebirth.

Three stars, three secrets, three futures.

I felt communion with Medea and Kryz, at one with the sangrael, aligned with my destiny. I experienced ultimate fulfillment and absolute loss. As the semblance of union faded, the planet's day seeped once again into my awareness. The sangrael had melded with the stone floor. Everything was different.

EIGHT

We took the wallcrawler back to the cliff station, took an autogyro back to Floating Island, and took Medea's shuttle back into space. Getting off-planet was a contemplative process given our experience of transcendence through the sangrael, but also vexing given the byzantine bureaucratic hoops we were forced to jump through. Once Medea's staryacht orbited into view, my buthu flyer tethered alongside, we still didn't have much to say. Our experience with the artifact, the Subite Effect, had gifted each of us with a momentary shared clairvoyance. We knew each other too well now—what each intended to do, where we each wanted to go, and what secrets we each had tried to keep—thanks to the sangrael.

Medea was what Pops called a conjure woman. A witch. She had been the most open about her plans, talking about her desire to find the galaxy's x-star. Now she had the galactic coordinates from the sangrael of a quark star orbiting the Milky Way on the fringes of the far Scutum-Centaurus Arm. But I also knew from the sangrael experience that she wanted to use the transmogrifying powers of that quark star to resurrect her dead sons. They were murdered because of her—by her actions if not her own hands—a deed that caused her endless sorrow. She would never have disclosed this to anyone, me and Kryz included, had it not been for the sangrael. But even as Medea contemplated outfitting an expedition to the quark star and using the sheer force of her will to bring her dead children back to life, the second sight afforded by the sangrael had exposed dark forces gathering to oppose her plans and take her down. Something primordial, vast, and powerful called the Othrysia were waiting for Medea to make her next move. They made the various adversaries that had been intent on hijacking the sangrael look like pikers by comparison. The Othrysia wanted Medea captured or killed, a contract motivating the attacks on us over our cargo as a pretext.

Kryz's desire to return to Bakru had been a deception by design, a matter of misdirection in replacing Bakru for her mythic Occulted Star. Bakru was real enough, but so was the occluded star called the Ðređuvda by the Rarjpujpar represented by her pendant. A cool subdwarf near their home system had been claimed and colonized more than a thousand years before and then outfitted with a slowly expanding megastructure. As the Dyson-style arcology took shape from swarm through bubble, net, and sphere to shell, all radiation from the Ðređuvda was gradually, deliberately reduced over the centuries, resulting in the star fading, then eventually "vanishing" altogether. The Rarji then used their completed Dyson shell to generate the space-time curvature to reposition the Ðređuvda to a new location, thus completely camouflaging their Occulted Star in a masterful bit of celestics. The thing is, humans—all non-Rarji sentience—weren't supposed to know about it. That's why Kryz dissembled, saying she wanted to return home to Bakru. Kryz still required reintegration into the hive after her accident, but that would happen as a matter of course on their hidden star, the Dyson shell's inner surface of which had apparently been constructed to surpass the architecture of Bakru by orders of magnitude.

The secret about my bracelet's eons-old Kalisthan star map and the location for Eden it supposedly revealed was perhaps the most closely kept because it was mine alone, shared neither by a history become mythology nor by a hive mind of billions. I'd half expected to find out nothing about Eden because it had been destroyed by a nearby supernova or because its star had been ejected from our galaxy or because it simply amounted to pure fantasy. Now I actually had the coordinates with the help of the sangrael's second sight. What's more, those coordinates tracked to somewhere in the Wiley Limit. I would need to run searches once back on *Skylark*, but odds were that Eden—if it existed—was a planet within the realm of human colonization. Anything within the Wiley Limit was fair game, according to our galactic charter, but there was always the matter of expense. So long as it didn't need to be terraformed or had an aboriginal population—in other words, as long as it was inhabitable but had not yet evolved its own sentience—Eden could be settled. I wasn't a farmer. I had no intention of becoming a farmer. But there was something to be said about mounting an exploratory flight to lay claim to whatever I found.

There was just one problem. Both Kryz and Medea knew about Eden. After all, I'd seen glimpses of Medea's two tearful, dying sons and the wondrous scalar architecture surrounding Kryz's Đređuvda star during our quasi-mystical session with the sangrael. I hoped they would keep my secret as I intended to keep theirs. The awe-infused high of our shared experience was slowly fading, and I was getting a little paranoid.

"I told you, said I'd still like a tour of Bakru," I reminded Kryz once she and I had returned to *Skylark*. "I hear it's one of the seven wonders of the galaxy. Nothing I know of can compare."

I winked, hoping that Kryz was familiar with that gesture.

"Bakru is our paradise," Kryz deadpanned. "I have no desire to pursue anyone else's myth of paradise. When can we depart for Bakru?"

"Soon as I clear it with our host," I answered with a smile.

Medea met me on the flying bridge of the *Colchis*. The stone grays and tans of Kapala rolled overhead. Her cat, Kate, nudged up against my ankles.

"My enemies are legion," Medea said, her protective insects restored, "many of whom I rightly earned through retaliation and retribution. I regret only one act of revenge, however. I didn't take kindly to my ex dumping me for another, so I eliminated my replacement."

I knew she was remorseless, but I was surprised she was also vindictive. "The Othrysia, they intend to destroy you when you get to the x-star. Am I right?"

"Which is why I'll have to conduct that business myself," she said. "No point in risking others for my follies. If I manage to get through the x-star trial unscathed, I am interested in your little project."

"I can't be certain that's entirely real," I said, suddenly leery of her attention. "I'll be running a blacktea search on the sangrael clues."

"If it turns out to be genuine, you could do with a sponsor. Even with all the money you earned on this job. I'm willing to be a silent partner or a no-strings-attached patron. Also, I have a little gift for your departure."

She reached into the pocket of her robe. Kate, who had been cleaning herself, perked up with a prickly sound. Medea held out an orange, black, and white ball of fur in her hands.

"Aye! It's a cat!" I exclaimed, cupping the suddenly purring creature in my hands.

"She's a calico." Medea gently scratched the kitten. "They're supposed to be good luck. You'll need it for your next adventure. You have the mythic tiger-by-the-tail with that one."

I took my leave of Medea with my new kitten. Kate had fascinated me from the start. I still had Kate's old cat supplies—litter box and scratching post—on *Skylark*. And Kryz was pleased we had a mascot in the calico cat for company on our short journey to Bakru. I initiated the search using the coordinates for the Kalisthani Eden. Xa brimmed with information—both fact and rumor—about four possible Shaktla sites nearby. I was irritated with its tendency to conflate the two, but I asked Xa to hold off reviewing what it found out until we had spaced. Kryz and I started preparations for departure without delay, taking on extra stores from the *Colchis* and running systems checks on *Skylark* in the control bubble. I refrained from opening a beer during the process.

The kitten slept nestled in my command chair. I performed my new rituals before departure—lighting chlawood incense and pouring a whiskey libation at the niche shrine. Blacktea chimed, coming back with findings of a nondescript, uninhabited star system—a G0-type star with six planets—at the sangrael's coordinates for Eden. I decided then to name the kitten Lilith.

MILKY WAY GALAXY MAP

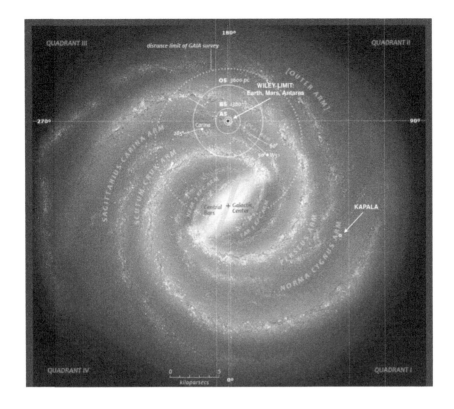

THE DEATH OF DAVID PICKETT

G.A. MATIASZ

This is a reprint of the novelette The Death of David Pickett published and distributed for free in September, 2018, as a digital download and limited print edition.

THE DEATH OF DAVID PICKETT

G.A. MATIASZ

For Kay
my broken grace

ONE

David Pickett's death upset a lot of people.

Jesse Steinfeld heard about it a little before noon on Sunday. He was in that state between sleep and wakefulness in his Mission District shoebox apartment when his smartphone rang with the incessant guitar thrum of Leonard Cohen's "Partisan." He fumbled for the phone on the headboard as a breeze played with drapes and sunlight.

"Yo," Jesse answered.

"Jesse, Dave Pickett is dead." The shrill voice at the other end belonged to Angie Markham. "Dave was driving back from Baja with friends when their car flipped. His abdomen was sliced open and he was bleeding out. The Mexican authorities tried to medevac him, but he was declared DOA at the hospital. They finally did it."

"Huh?" He grunted, still chasing the tail end of a dream. "Who did what to whom?"

"Assassinated Dave," Angie said. "CIA, FBI, NSA, AFL-CIO, whoever. Haven't you been listening?"

Jesse hung up. He'd never liked Angie's sharp, accusatory way of speaking, even when he'd had a brief relationship with her two years ago. He eased out of his double bed and walked three steps into the kitchenette, where he turned on the programmed coffeemaker. He walked a half-dozen steps back the other way into the bathroom for a quick shower and shave, washing away the remnants of last night's Retromingent concert at the Korova Bar.

Jesse knew David from the city's music scene and the Bay Area's political milieu. They'd met, in passing, at the Skeleton Club back when he was still sleeping with Angie. At a party, happening, or concert he was aware of Pickett's crew as the storm on the horizon and of David as the eye of that storm. Jesse had stumbled upon a provocative rally turned street fight staged by David and his cohorts in support of bike messengers' rights a year ago, and had purchased six doses of a powerful designer psychedelic, jamrax, from David at Stumpy's six months ago. But Jesse still considered him only an acquaintance at best.

The aroma of Colombian coffee saturated the apartment by the time he had toweled off. He poured fragrant coffee into an oversized Foamy-the-Squirrel mug before he dressed from a tiny closet in the minuscule combination living/dining room. He put on black Converse high-tops, narrow black jeans, classic Catholic Spit black-and-white band T-shirt, and a black Dickies hoodie, then took his coffee onto the fire escape and relaxed.

David Pickett had been a fixture of Bay Area progressive politics for the past decade or so. He had a solid reputation as a community organizer, labor militant, and political powerhouse. Yet David's notoriety in edge politics was even more pronounced as a commie impresario, a left of the Left raconteur, and an anarcho-provocateur. He was the founder of What's Left?— an extremely popular website, a volatile social networking site, and a print-version zine with a circulation approaching two million. His powerful speech during the "Fuck Work, Fuck Borders" conference three years ago had gone viral, making him a rising star of the emerging revolutionary Synarky movement. And his popular podcast series "FSU" averaged more than eight million unique monthly subscribers.

Jesse soaked in the afternoon sun as he gradually caffeinated himself. The weather pattern was standard for San Francisco in midsummer; the overcast had burned off, leaving blue skies. The gray fog bank out past Twin Peaks looked like a line of surf threatening to break. The smells from a taqueria down the block wafted up to the fire escape. The thirty-six-ounce mug, having declared "Squirrelly Rage" to the world, was half empty.

David Pickett had also founded Drinkers United International, an anti-union of sorts inspired by Oscar Wilde's quip that "Work is the curse of the drinking classes." Under his leadership, DUI gained prominence through its tireless relief work for and armed defense of the poor and homeless after the 2021 earthquake. Its various front activities included mobile hiring halls and interest-specific social clubs.

DUI became infamous, however, for a number of wildcat actions involving software coders, fast food workers, day laborers, sex workers, and the like—actions with a flair for the spectacular that often turned violent. The violent assault on the Bohemian Grove in Monte Rio by DUI was the stuff of legend.

Jesse rinsed the empty mug in the sink and set up next morning's drip, then took the stairs down to the street. He had a freelance archiving job tomorrow but nothing that interfered with his boho lifestyle. First stop, Sam's Sons Deli for their Reuben sandwich. Second stop was Stumpy's Pub for a pint or three of Belgian ale. Jesse suspected that David's comrades and friends, perhaps even some of his frenemies and enemies, were already beginning to gather at Stumpy's. David's political milieu was Jesse's by acquaintance and happenstance. He started on a refreshing walk up Guerrero, past the homeless encampment stirring to life at the corner of 24th.

After the 2021 tech bubble collapse, out-of-work techies fled the Mission District, which effectively halted the neighborhood's contentious gentrification. But the popular movement to declare autonomy for the Mission District, and to call itself the "Mission Commune," had so far failed. The City of San Francisco disregarded petitions, referenda, elections, demonstrations, and street violence. Instead, it increased surveillance and harassment of the indigent and destitute, especially around rich areas. The Liberty Hill Historic District ahead was just such a tony neighborhood of mini-mansions and upscale condos in the midst of the Mission that escalated in wealth from east to west until it was virtually a walled enclave catercorner to Mission Dolores Park. No surprise that its residents paid dearly for a variety of private security services to protect themselves from the rabble living and breathing a mere street corner away. Top among them were patrols by unmanned aerial vehicles.

Jesse saw the drone whir around the corner from 22nd Street onto Guerrero toward Alvarado bearing logos for Ambassador Security and Bank of America. "Fucking PUD," he said under his breath. UAVs were often called PUDs, an acronym for the public—or private—urban drones deployed with increasing frequency in and around the Bay Area. Like the word drone itself, PUD was a somewhat rude term that had entered the vernacular. People who lived in the Mission had an explosive antipathy for PUDs, public or private, which went beyond the general dislike for being watched in public spaces. Except during riots, however, few people messed with heavily armed law-enforcement UAVs. Private urban drones were another matter, even though more of the private ones were allowed to carry and use weapons, thanks to California's castle doctrine. This one did.

The reason that the drone ventured beyond its turf was not immediately evident. The response to its intrusion was immediate and violent. Two powerful green lasers from farther down Guerrero pinned the PUD, barely visible in daylight, yet effective in causing the drone to react. Instead of retreating, however, the UAV held its ground, hovering above the LED streetlight.

"Cease and desist," a mechanical male voice boomed from the drone. *"You are in violation of section —"*

Five more lasers targeted the drone. Rioters used wrist-rocket slingshots, power catapults, stone bows, and human power to hurl rocks, pieces of brick, bottles, marbles, ball bearings, nuts, and bolts at the drone. Blinded by lasers, pummeled by projectiles, again the drone refused to retreat, for whatever reason.

"Cease and desis—" The PUD crackled, lost the final consonant, listed, then dropped a meter. A distant police siren sounded. The drone got off two wild shots before spiraling down to smash into two parked cars.

A roar of triumph greeted the PUD's crash and two dozen street people ran for the drone's twisted wreckage. An SUV with Ambassador Security markings skidded into the intersection and three men brandishing guns piled out. But the crowd brandished firearms, too. The dozen individuals not holding guns began dragging the broken drone down the street, screaming *"Our streets!"* and *"Back the fuck off!"*

The crowd moved toward a pickup truck that had just pulled up. Three armed men hauled the drone into the truck as the security guards yelled, *"Stop, motherfuckers!"* By the time two cop cars arrived on the scene, the truck sped off and the other armed civilians melted into the neighborhood with the rest of the crowd, leaving both public and private cops frustrated, talking to each other.

Jesse left as police reinforcements arrived. He circumvented the confrontation's dénouement with Sam's Sons Deli once again in mind, replaying the fight as he picked up his sandwich. A flock of iridescent green-and-red parrots squawked in the palm trees above him as he walked along Dolores.

Stumpy's was a dive bar, pure and proud, in the Lower Haight east of the Wiggle. Featuring a selection of sixty-plus draft and ninety-plus bottled beers, it had been unofficial headquarters for DUI, and David Pickett, for the past four years. Angie Markham also kept propaganda at the bar for her more staid Precarious Union, which was a direct reaction to DUI and to David's bold, rabble-rousing political style. The rivalry between them often tried loyalties. Angie was eighteen years older than Jesse, and their relationship had been rocky. She drank heavily, and was often passed out by evening. He found her in her apartment one night raving, frantically brushing off imaginary spiders, desperately searching for her car keys and the money to buy more alcohol. Shaken and unnerved, never having seen a case of the DTs, Jesse nevertheless had the presence of mind to hide her purse.

Blatz's "Fuk Shit Up" blasted from the open door in the red-and-black facade. Jesse entered the dark bar, the atmosphere stinking of beer, sweat, cigarettes, and vomit, found a stool at the bar, and placed the sandwich on the worn wooden countertop.

"What'll it be?" the heavily tattooed bartender asked.

"Pint of Lucifer," Jesse said, and unwrapped his sandwich. As he suspected, a sizable crowd in the back was talking up David Pickett's death and the radical demo in Dolores Park later that evening. That and the takedown of the PUD. He didn't recognize anyone so he started eating in peace. The pint arrived. Sam's Sons' Reuben Combo was perfection. The pint was beyond perfection. When Jesse looked back up, Stenny Amps had materialized on the barstool next to him.

"Long time, Jesse," Stenny said. Jesse noted the covetous glance toward the sandwich and the lengthy longing look at the beer. The stench of Stenny's crusty clothing assaulted his nose. "Free Speech" by Citizen Fish played in the background.

"How's the band going?" Jesse asked, quickly draining the pint. "What's the name again?"

"Dead Girls Can't Say No," Stenny said, and watched as Jesse started in on the other half of the Reuben. "We've got a gig next Friday, at the Chatsubo."

"Good to hear it," he said between bites. "So, what's your take on David Pickett?"

"Nothing to say," Stenny said, with a dismissive wave of a hand. "He was off-roading with a bunch of his Drinking United cadre in the Sonoran Desert. Fancy Yamaha motocross bikes. He took a spill, sustained a lot of damage from rocks, had a lot of internal injuries. Died from an internal hemorrhage in the abdomen. End of story."

"Nothing untoward?"

"Not a goddamn nefarious thing about it."

"Wow." Jesse finished up the sandwich. "Glad to hear the real story. Lots of rumors going round."

"Well, I got the genuine report," Stenny said. "You heard about taking down that PUD? I was right there—"

"I was half a block away, watching the whole thing." Jesse crumpled the sandwich paper and stuffed it into the bag.

"Oh, wasn't that something." Stenny offered a weak grin, then dodged Jesse's eyes. "Ya know, I'm a bit strapped for cash until our show, and I was wondering—"

"Hold that thought," Jesse said, and stood up from his stool, abandoning an empty pint glass and crumbs. "I'll be back. Got to take a wicked leak."

When Jesse got to the unisex bathrooms at mid-bar and turned back, Stenny had evaporated. *Fucking moocher.* There wasn't much of a line, and he didn't have much of a pee. Just as he was about to turn back for another beer, Ari Moser came out of one of the toilets.

"Well, well, if it isn't Jesse the Zionist," Ari said, with a sly smile. "How's Romi these days?"

Romi was Jesse's pretty younger sister whom Ari had been eager to sex up a while back. The man's desire to sleep with her had been inflamed by her making *aliya* and then joining up with the IDF for her mandatory military service, where she served in the joint US/Israeli nuclear operation Wrath of God.

"Romi is out of the Army," Jesse said. "She's married and has a baby."

"Shame," Ari mused. "Buy you a beer?"

They were still on the edge of the scrum in which Pickett's death was discussed and debated. Amenity's "This Is Our Struggle" roared over the sound system. Cigarette smoke rolled from one end of the bar to the other. Ari had a Racer 5, Jesse a Black Damnation VI. They faced the mirror behind the bar, with Ari clocking every passing female.

"Too bad about the fourth Intifada," Ari said, after a gulp. "What with Hezbollah still mired deep in what's left of Syria and the rest of the Middle East reduced to nuclear chaos, it looks like Gaza is going to get razed."

"Dude, I'm not playing that game," Jesse said, and drank. "You win. I concede. You're a better anti-Zionist Jew than I am."

"Hey, dude," Ari smirked. "No more pissing contest, okay? Your sister is still one smoking hot chick, Israeli or not. Married or not."

"So, what do you make of Pickett's death?"

"Way I heard it, he was down in Baja, working with the PRD-affiliated Authentic Labor Front." Ari watched the ass of a voluptuous redhead as she sashayed toward the bathroom. "And there was something definitely not kosher about his demise."

"How so?"

"Well, for one thing, it appears that the Arellano-Félix Cartel had a hand in helping the Federales run him off the road. For another, no hospital on either side of the border has any record of admitting him, alive or dead. For a third, US authorities are remarkably reticent about the circumstances around Dave's death."

"So, you're saying this was political."

"No doubt about it," Ari said, finishing his pint. He caught the wink of a stunning brunette in the mirror from behind him. "So, dude, gotta run. Give Romi my regards."

Jesse ordered a dark Armageddon ale and considered what he'd been told. Two for and one against David Pickett's death being political. And yet he considered the odds to be even, he thought as he systematically worked on the pint. Stenny Amps was a freeloader and a bum and loved to exaggerate his own exploits. But he was not prone to wild conspiracy theories. Ari Moser's more reasoned, if darker, analysis of the political implications of Pickett's passing was more than offset by the tinfoil-hat idiocy of Angie Markham's alcohol-fueled conspiratorial ruminations. Speaking of which...

"Stay fucking right there, Jesse Steinfeld!" Angie's piercing screech cut through the dense barroom din, even as L7's "This Ain't the Summer of Love" blared above it all. She was small, barely over five feet, but Jesse could see her from across the room trying to shove her way through the unyielding throng. He guzzled the rest of his beer in record time as he lost sight of her, but he could still hear her. *"Don't you fucking leave!"*

He ducked down from his stool, then wove his way, crouching, toward the dazzling light of the open door. An agonizing minute later, he reached the door, the day, and freedom. He looked back to see Angie standing at the doorway, distraught. Jesse raced down the sidewalk and turned the corner on Fillmore. He ran past the grocery store murals, past Laussat Street, and past more murals adorning a Cambodian restaurant. Only then did he stop to catch his breath.

It was late afternoon, approaching evening. His smartphone kept ringing, so he turned it off. An airbus wheezed down Fillmore. He grabbed a ride by swiping his phone's Clipper app and settled into a seat next to an elderly man dressed in a suit and tie and reading audibly from a Bible. Jesse was enjoying the effects of his three pints of strong ale, so when he switched to a Muni train at Church headed for the park and the demonstration, he was feeling no pain. The sun was nestling into that fog bank above Twin Peaks.

The Muni rattled up along the west side of Dolores Park, giving Jesse a view of the rally in progress on the green soccer fields. He disembarked. Parrots wheeled overhead, chirping and shrieking. He saw Toby Barnabas get off the train, too. He was a tall lanky Mohawked man he knew from hanging around the periphery of Pickett's militant circles. He was dressed in black with a leather jacket sporting the familiar Mohawked skulls of The Exploited's *Fuck the System* album. Toby walked, chatting with his über-Goth girlfriend, Cynthia, "Tank Girl" on her leather jacket. They did not see Jesse.

Jesse didn't close in on the rally. Not right away. First he bought four Boston cream donuts. Then he circled around the rally, listening to the speeches as darkness descended. Perhaps four hundred people were standing around. A cop drone lazily wheeled above the gathering. Unlike the mob that immediately took down the encroaching PUD earlier in the day, an air of impending trouble hung over the crowd. No fan of anarchist smashy-smashy, Jesse nevertheless felt compelled to stay by the threat of sweet violence. He thought he saw Ari Moser among the rabble, but lost sight of him. A wind had started to whip up, blowing snippets of words and sentences away. Much of the rest echoed unintelligibly around the park, along with Public Enemy's "Party for Your Right to Fight."

"...*David Pickett was an enemy of the state, a target of every American police, security, and military agency...*"

The gathering was overwhelmingly young, about evenly male and female, and dressed principally in black. There was a pungent smell of marijuana and tobacco throughout those assembled. People kept arriving as Jesse stayed at the margin. Toby and Cynthia were in the thick of it.

"...*ickett's legacy was to stand for the helpless, to stand with the downtrodden, to stand against the rich and powerful. David Pickett was a friend of the impoverished multitude and an enemy of the wealthy few. D...*"

The crowd had swollen to well over a thousand and many were masked up. It was fully dark now. The clinking of glass bottles accompanied the smell of gasoline. A tight knot of miscreants surrounded Toby and snickered at one of his jokes. Toby flashed something, quickly and surreptitiously, then hid it in his jacket.

"...*time to avenge our fallen friend, our murdered brother, our assassinated comrade! It's time to wreak our havoc against the cops, against capital and state, against all the powers-that-be! It's time to MOVE!*"

Hoodies came up, balaclavas were donned, black bandannas were tied around faces. Full black-bloc mode. And the mob surged toward 18th and Dolores, toward rows of businesses, toward the nearest police station.

"*One, two, three, four; this is fucking class war!*"

Glow sticks, flashlights, and lasers pierced the gloom. Here and there, a fiery torch burned. Jesse joined the crowd at the tail end as the crowd occupied the middle of the street. A second PUD joined the first, and both kept tabs on the march.

"*Racist, sexist, anti-gay; SFPD go away!*"

Tires popped, and car windows shattered. Car alarms howled and squealed. Bystanders watched the unruly march from upper-story windows. Gas masks appeared. Lasers lanced up from the protest onto the UAVs, the crowd hoping to keep the drones blinded.

"*What do we want?*"

"*Dead cops!*"

"*When do we want them?*"

"*Now!*"

Jesse could see the crowd marching toward the Mission Street Police Station. He moved to the sidewalk, where he watched the police quickly reinforce the line of officers behind the standing wall of steel barricades, between the station and the mob. The black-clad rabble roared in response.

"*Whose streets?*"

"*Our streets!*"

"*Fuck the police!*"

The mob used paint bombs, bricks, bottles, rocks, metal hardware, and debris, primarily against the station and secondarily toward the multiplying drones. Dressed in fire-resistant riot suits, the cops raised their shields and sprayed the crowd with tear gas. Pivoting UAVs also let loose a rain of pepper bombs and flash-bang grenades. By then, Jesse had moved to the opposite sidewalk and pushed his way down Valencia, past the riot proper and out of range of the gas. The second wave involved smoke bombs to obscure the mob and people hurling Molotov cocktails, until the line of cops appeared engulfed in flames.

One PUD veered away and crash-landed behind the station. But the shields and fire-retardant uniforms, plus a constant dry spray of sodium bicarbonate from nozzles in the station, rapidly contained the inferno.

Then the police launched liquid pepper spray and high-power microwave weapons, designed to dispense excruciating pain as subcutaneous heat or intracranial sound. The HPM antennas swiveled down from the roof and powered up with subsonics. The air above the riot rippled ominously. The mini-insurrection redoubled their attack— the projectiles, the paint and smoke bombs, and the Molotovs—plus their ace: glitter bombs. Thrown high into the air, the fine metal glitter bombs exploded and holy hell broke loose. Lightning streamers, sheets of lightning, ball lightning erupted between falling glitter and the microwave weapons in violent claps and crackles until the microwave devices short-circuited and the police station roof caught fire. Two PUDs shot sparks and careened into the building.

The battle for the station proved only a diversion, however. As soon as the glitter bombs went off, the cops had to respond to their burning building. The organized assault turned into absolute chaos as hordes of black-clad rioters ran into the heart of Valencia Street's restaurant row. Cars, stores, windows, restaurants, pedestrians—everything was fair game. Diners, indoors and out, ran for their lives. The sound of breaking glass punctuated the night. Smoke bombs blew up, roping the night air with thick, acrid clouds. Rioters brandishing pipes and wooden clubs felled gawkers and bystanders. Gasoline bombs blossomed into conflagrations. Broken glass carpeted the streets.

Jesse ran through the spreading anarchy hoping to escape it. He coughed, gasped, and his eyes watered. At 22nd, he froze. The plate-glass windows were broken, but the blinking neon signage— "Spencer's"—wasn't. A burly crew-cut man, dressed in chef's apron, barred the door to the partially trashed, empty restaurant. The restaurateur held a pump-action shotgun across his chest. "Come one step further, assholes," he bellowed. "*And you'll be eating this!*"

The crowd surrounded him in a half-circle, taunting him, but from a respectful distance. Suddenly, a tall, lanky, Mohawked man stepped into the space between them. He wore a black balaclava, and his black leather jacket bore a logo: *The Exploited. Fuck the System.* "Here's for all those shitty wages you paid me and my fellow workers! Here's for David Pickett!" He yanked a Glock from his jacket and fired 9mm rounds into the restaurateur. *One. Two. Three. Four.*

TWO

Bloody sunrise seeped along the eastern sky. Jesse huddled on the fire escape outside his apartment. To the northwest, the sights and sounds of the riot faded with the new day.

He hadn't slept all night. Terrible images burned his memory. The gun, flashing under streetlights. The four terrible shots. Each shot loud, tracing murder through the dark air. The shooter's arm recoiling. The restaurateur collapsing. The smell of cordite. The smell of blood. Blood flowing across the sidewalk. The shotgun lying on the sidewalk.

Jesse ran. Everybody ran. He didn't know how or when he got back home to his apartment. He just remembered cowering in the dark. Terrified. Crying. Praying.

The morning was painfully clear. Not a shred of overcast in the sharp blue sky, not a wisp of fog over Twin Peaks. The sun sluiced golden over East Bay's hills. Jesse unsteadily grabbed the railing to his fire escape and pulled himself up. Trembling, he stumbled into his apartment, fumbled for the light in his kitchenette, and turned on the coffeemaker. He noticed the vaguely familiar rumpled waxy bag on the kitchen counter. Awful recollections flooded his brain as he opened the bag. It was filled with crumbled donut cake, flaked chocolate icing, and smeared vanilla custard. The stink punched him in the nose. Jesse leaned over the sink and vomited. He continued to throw up until it became uncontrolled retching, then dry heaves. He collapsed onto the linoleum and clutched his aching stomach.

He got back onto his feet, weak and shaking. He turned on the faucet and rinsed away the puke until the fresh smell of coffee replaced the rank odor of barf.

Time to get out into the morning and to the day's job. Jesse showered, hosed the vomit from his mouth, put on an orange Burning Bush T-shirt and a gray sweatshirt, and hefted an empty thermos. He bought copies of the *SF Chronicle* and *San Jose Mercury News* and drank half of the coffee before settling onto a bench at the Mission Playground and Pool. A police UAV floated along the street. "Local Militant's Death Triggers Mission Riot," the *Chronicle* proclaimed, whereas the *Mercury News'* headline was more blunt: "One Dead, 326 Injured, 144 Arrested in Anarchist Riot." He read the reports on the Valencia Street riot, including the opinion pieces about the incompetence of the police to protect anyone or prevent damage to local businesses, then ripped out the articles on David Pickett's death. Folding the crisp pages into his back pocket, he discarded the remainder of the newspaper. Jesse needed time to analyze the news items, with more than caffeine to fuel him. His favorite cafe, Hopwell's, was down the block.

"Fill 'er up," he said as he presented the waitress his thermos, then looked at the menu. "I want the breakfast special."

He switched on his smartphone while waiting for his meal. Forty-two messages, seventy-one texts. Eighteen of the voice messages were from Angie Markham, the first ten ranging from "Where the fuck are you?" to "You asshole!" Four from her were simple hang-ups. Twelve texts out of twenty were of a similar nature, including three all-caps messages: "THEY MURDERED DAVID PICKETT!" Her tone changed abruptly after he'd fled from Stumpy's. The calls and texts that followed begged him to call her back and please forgive her, pleading, "We need to talk" and "We can work through this." Jesse felt a pang in his heart, but he deleted them all, then switched his phone to vibrate. Best to keep a meditative state of mind, he thought, and avoid confrontation. And nasty messages.

When breakfast arrived, he concentrated on the food, savoring each bite between each breath. Only when he'd cleaned his plate, only when he'd paid the check, only when he'd stepped back into the burnished San Francisco morning did the terrors of the night before return. He felt oddly refreshed, however, for not having slept in nearly twenty-four hours and returned to the apartment for his equipment.

"Shit," Jesse mumbled when he reached his door at the top of the stairs. He pulled the card from between door and jamb. Beneath the SFPD logo, the card read "Investigator Michael Van Cornin" above the usual address and telephone contact information. On the back, a cellphone number had been written, in pen. "Shit, fuck, piss," Jesse said.

Jesse snagged a notebook, pens, markers, label maker, and his first-generation Apple Fetch, which he stuffed into his knapsack before rushing out the door. He took the direct route over to Valencia and then north until he was surrounded by drones, idling cop cars and conferring police officers—and rolls of yellow crime tape. The sidewalk around Spencer's Restaurant was completely sealed off for a quarter block in each direction. The Mission Street Police Station was open for business, despite obvious signs of damage. He tried to look inconspicuous even as he minutely observed his surroundings. Once past all the wreckage, he turned east at the homeless camp on 16th Street and walked to 2930 16th.

The old, four-story, red brick building occupied much of the block. Known as the Redstone Labor Temple, or simply the Redstone Building, the structure was home to scores of labor unions, nonprofit organizations, and various and sundry artists. Jesse entered using a duplicate key and a combination to the Digilock. He had access thanks to his friendship with graphic designer and silkscreen artist Marco Loyola, who shared a fourth floor, west-facing office with an artist collective calling itself Chicanosaurus. Once in the funky, poster-and-mural-encrusted lobby, he climbed the stairs. He tread carefully down the fourth-floor hall because Marco's fellow collective members were not very welcoming of Jesse's white ass. The door chimed with the opening notes of Victor Jara's "Venceremos." Fortunately, the musty office was unoccupied.

Jesse had studied Library and Information Science at City College, interned in Digital Archiving at UC Berkeley's Bancroft Library, and had remained sporadically employed ever since. He'd met Marco through the William James Work Association, a worker-run temp agency operated by David Pickett's DUI, at the onset of the Marco's multiple sclerosis. Jesse started working for him scanning, digitizing, massaging, and cataloguing the artist's work and papers using Photoshop software and Macintosh computers. Marco used the office space primarily for storage of his prints and files, as advanced MS now kept him confined to his tiny Inner Mission cottage.

Jesse had spent hours taking in the contents of the office while working for Marco. The floor-to-ceiling filing system that took up most of one wall; flat file drawers and vertical hanging racks, constructed of varnished, weathered oak. The iconography in photography, silkscreening, painting, lithography, even graffiti depicted historical political, religious, and artistic figures from Spain and the Americas. He spread out the contents of his knapsack over the work table by the window, then lifted the window shades, mindful not to disturb the reflector telescope positioned with a focus on the BART plaza a block away. Pen-and-ink drawings painstakingly rendering aspects of the plaza were taped on the window jambs near the telescope.

The Fetch picked up a Wi-Fi signal immediately and Marco's password worked. The office boombox had a mixtape of *corridos* and *norteños* he played low. He put in a solid two hours on Marco's archiving project. In the process of scrupulously labeling and alphabetizing a cardboard box full of document CDs, he discovered a cryptic item. One CD in a worn white sleeve bore a dingy Post-it that read: "HOOLIGAN-X = D PICKETT?" CDs were antiquated technology and electronic players were ancient history, so he was at a loss. He put the sleeve and its contents into the knapsack before turning his attention to Pickett and the riot. He looked up a number of local news websites, laid out the pages ripped from the *Chronicle* and *Mercury News*, opened the notebook, uncapped the pen, and started to write. The sun claimed more and more of the table as it edged into late afternoon. An hour and ten minutes later, Jesse had three paragraphs written in the notebook and a new mixtape of Latinx resistance music in the boombox.

Notwithstanding some intriguing aspects to Pickett's biography, it was how he died—whether it was an accident or murder—that mattered to Jesse now. Pickett died Saturday, July 15, at approximately 5:20 pm, after the Ford station wagon he was driving overturned on Highway 1, ten kilometers north of Mulegé. According to the *Chronicle*, Pickett and his four companions were returning from a scuba expedition at Bahia de Concepcion when the car and the dirt bike trailer it was towing flipped shortly after noon. Except for minor scrapes, none of the other passengers were seriously injured. Pickett's injuries were far more serious—his abdomen cut open and his intestines perforated. The *Mercury News* claimed that a sixth person, a local fisherman and guide named Arnulfo Cassias, had also been present but uninjured.

Pickett's injury warranted, first, transportation by helicopter to Hospital Angeles Tijuana, and then to UC San Diego Medical Center, where he was pronounced DOA. First on the scene, the Federales conveyed David to the hospital and arrested his diving buddies before ultimately transferring custody of Pickett to the California Highway Patrol. The CHP rushed him to San Diego. Somewhere in the midst of all of this, the FBI got involved.

The reporting was incomplete, inconsistent, and secondhand. So far, no evidence had surfaced for or against the involvement of these law enforcement agencies in Pickett's death. There was also no information as to whether the diving excursion was business or pleasure. The *Chronicle* cast doubt on the FBI's contention that Pickett's expedition had been innocuous. The *Mercury News* had little to say for or against the FBI, but pointed out that David's diving companions were still in jail. Their diving equipment, three motocross bikes, and two duffle bags of undisclosed contraband from their dives at Bahia de Concepcion had been confiscated.

Jesse shook his head over the mounting contradictions between official news accounts and between the news and the rumors he'd heard. When David Pickett's death became known to San Francisco's locals, last night's riot had erupted. The Bay Area media was heavily criticizing the SFPD for failing to anticipate the mayhem at the police station, the wholesale destruction to the Valencia Street business district, and the murder of Spencer's restaurateur, Samuel Barbier. Grainy videos of the murder from a PUD were in continuous rotation on every TV outlet. The SFPD had a BOLO out for the murderer as well as a call for witnesses and any information related to the murder.

Jesse reviewed the information he'd written up and remembered the CD when persistent noise from the waning afternoon outside intervened. Seven cop drones converged on the airspace over the BART plaza with a growing clatter. He popped the lens covers off the telescope and looked through the pre-positioned instrument. Six Mission District Latinos stood, clustered, in the middle of the plaza, as scores of cops, in plain clothes and in uniform, carefully approached. The cops had their guns leveled. Two more PUDs whirred over. Four of the youngsters started to raise their arms. Was that a bottle of water or a gun in an upraised hand? Suddenly, shooting rang from the plaza. "Holy shit," Jesse breathed, but didn't take his eye from the lens. Volley after volley shattered the sunlit day. When the gunshots stopped, all six young men were lying motionless on the square. There was blood everywhere.

He shoveled everything into the knapsack, dropped the window shade, turned off the music, and made sure the office door was shut and locked before sprinting down the stairs. He was at the BART station within five minutes, but by then there was a full-on police cordon in place, cops and police cars holding the line, with more men and vehicles arriving every moment. The early evening sky was jammed with UAVs.

Jesse hovered around the periphery of the police barrier. However, it soon became clear that there was no getting near where the police killed the six young men. The crowd outside the cordon was growing larger. And angrier. He walked south on Mission, stunned and staggered. Police sirens wailed. He climbed his apartment stairs, tossed his knapsack onto the couch, and eased out his window to stand on the fire escape in the cool of the evening. The orange sun got entangled with Sutro Towers on its way toward bloody sunset.

He remembered three grandparents, an aunt, and two cousins who died, as had two high school classmates, a college professor, and now David Pickett. But he hadn't personally witnessed any of their deaths and now, within twenty-four hours, Jesse had seen seven people shot dead. Gunned down. Murdered. He turned on his smartphone but his fingers shook too much to use the tiny virtual keyboard. So he re-entered his apartment, switched on the Fetch, and activated its communication apps.

There were seven additional voice messages, eight more texts, and an email from Angie, all of which he deleted without opening. Jesse had ended their relationship, a kind of death, but a gutless one. He'd never called it quits; he just stopped seeing or contacting her. He wasn't proud of his behavior, but he couldn't yield to the pull of his heart. The remaining messages—thirty-eight voice mails, sixty-six texts, and twenty-one emails—fell into several categories. Eight were wrong numbers/addresses and thirty-odd were advertisements. The rest were an assortment of messages, texts, and emails from friends and acquaintances about David Pickett's death. Asking "Hey, did you hear…" and "What do you think about…" Some "Sorry about…" and "Hope you're…". He'd dealt with all the emails and texts and was working through the last third of the voice messages when he heard: "This is Investigator Van Cornin with the Homicide Detail. I need to speak to a Jesse Jacob Steinfeld at his earliest convenience."

How did Van Cornin know his smartphone number? Did he have to worry about Van Cornin hounding him at his apartment? He opened a browser on his Fetch to look up Van Cornin's SFPD biography. Jesse saw on the social media newsfeeds that a demonstration, Occupy the

Mission, was set for Wednesday at Dolores Park. He continued deleting phone messages. The last message raised the hairs on the back of his neck.

"Jesse, this is David Pickett, calling you from beyond the grave." The voice sounded loud and present, inflected with David's signature gravel and a bit of a chuckle. "You and I haven't been real good friends. Didn't know each other well at all, matter of fact. But, now that I'm on the other side, I need you to take care of that thing with Toby for me. It ain't cool, what he did in my name."

The voice on the message hung up. Jesse sat, dumbfounded. What kind of shitty joke was this?

He kept the message but turned the phone to vibrate. Time to visit Kevin Farley. He'd contracted Kevin's services when he'd gotten himself into a jam. Jesse handled other people's data as a digital archivist, but in trying to cut corners and save costs, he'd let a client's work get hijacked and held for ransom. Kevin had recovered the stolen data without paying the ransom. But Farley wasn't answering his phone and his website only offered appointments for the next day, starting at 11 a.m. Jesse took the first available appointment.

Between thinking about the call from Van Cornin and the one supposedly from David Pickett, Jesse's fears kicked in. He ran down to the corner taqueria, Goyaałé, for a burrito and the corner liquor store for three bottles of Chimay Tripel, but neither food nor alcohol nor several hits of prime indica bud alleviated his anxieties.

THREE

Jesse awoke the next morning, showered, and downed copious amounts of coffee. To jeans and T-shirt he added a "Groucho Marxist" sweatshirt. He switched on his Fetch for news of the deepening turmoil in China and NATO's counter to the Ukrainian/Moldovan invasion of Romania, only to quickly turn it off. He ignored his new phone messages, the preponderance of them from Angie. Instead he hefted the knapsack, with Fetch, CD, and notebook inside, locked his apartment, and ran down the stairs to his apartment building two at a time, hoping not to run into representatives of the SFPD on their way up.

Kevin lived in a three-story Victorian house in the heart of the Inner Mission, surrounded by sketchy public housing and colorful Precita Eyes murals. During the heyday of Silicon Valley, Kevin made his nut and then some, more than enough to retire and purchase the Victorian. He lived alone. A server farm occupied the air-conditioned basement, supporting his various and sundry web enterprises. The second-floor rooms had been modified to accommodate a high-grade hydroponic marijuana farm—insulated for moisture, heat, and light; vented and filtered through the walls and attic. Solar panels covered the roof, and a biofuel/electricity generator and windmill shared the backyard with a chicken coop and rabbit hutch. Kevin had the ground and third floors for his residence, the whole structure properly defended by bars, alarm systems, armed robotics, 24-hour mobile surveillance, and an on-call private security patrol.

It was approaching noon when Jesse knocked. The porch was sunny and spacious. As he waited, listening to birds chirping and chickens clucking, he sensed that various surveillance systems were checking him out.

"Come on in," Kevin said through a speaker as the front door unlocked. "I'm upstairs, in CentCom."

The door closed and locked behind him. The dark entryway was spotlighted at the far end. The lighting anticipated him as he progressed through the living room, up three flights of stairs, and down a hall. The door to CentCom, short for Central Command, was up another short flight of stairs and wide open.

"Jesse, my boy." Kevin swiveled his sizable bulk in an Aeron chair modified for his mass. "What can I do you for?"

Kevin was obese by any standard. Dressed in a light-gray sweatshirt, dark-gray sweatpants, and unlaced silver-gray track shoes, he was surrounded by a dozen flickering computer screens. Central Command occupied the top floor of a turret tower running the house's northwest corner to just above roof level, with panopticon windows providing a panoramic view of the Mission. Jesse slung the knapsack onto a table near the door.

"I need your investigatory talents," Jesse said, and took the only other chair in the room. "I've got a mystery here that's bordering on the bizarre."

"Gotcha." Kevin smiled.

"What's it going to cost me?"

"First things first. Tell me your problem."

Jesse pulled out his smartphone and replayed the David Pickett message. Ambient air conditioning kept the atmosphere odorless. "I want you to tell me as much as possible about this message. Who sent it? Was it really from David, or did somebody engineer a fake message? And, I know this would be beyond your abilities, but can you hazard a guess as to why somebody would want to send me such a message?"

"Wow." Kevin extended his hand and closed his pudgy fingers on the phone. He searched through several cables next to him, pulled one up, and attached it to the smartphone. "Mind if I port your phone? I'm first going to record the message, then I'm going to access your provider. This should take a minute or two."

In five minutes, the screen in front of Kevin was divided into several quick-reference video panels. He didn't like working to music, so the sounds of the neighborhood mingled gently with the hum of electronics and the clack of his keyboard.

"Okay, let me see here." Kevin perused the screen. "I'll be able to run some diagnostics, both on the recorded message and on the message as routed through your provider to your smartphone. If you want me to continue, we can discuss payment."

"By all means."

"My basic rate is one fifty for thirty minutes." He smiled at Jesse. "For friends, it's a hundred. That's for any part of a half hour."

"Give me an hour, to start."

"Right," Kevin said, and turned back to the screen. "Let's start with the recording. There are plenty of apps out there we can run this recording through to verify its veracity. Or lack thereof."

Kevin fast-forwarded through scores of podcasts and YouTube recordings of Pickett's copious speeches, talks, lectures, monologues, debates, spiels, and the like, processing them before running the smartphone message through the same software.

"You participating in the *huelga general* tomorrow?" Kevin asked as he worked.

"The what?"

"The general strike. To protest killing the homeboys and David Pickett."

"I haven't been paying much attention lately," he deflected. "By the way, can you help me with something else? Something minor. Can you tell me what's on this?"

Jesse handed Kevin the sleeve and CD, minus the Post-it.

"Talk about stone knives and bearskins." Kevin examined the disk before feeding it into a computer slot. "There are twenty-three PDFs here of what appear to be legal documents."

"Can you print them out?"

"Will do," Kevin said, then pointed to a far corner of his desk, once again engrossed in work. "Printer's there."

Jesse picked up the papers from the printer and the CD from Kevin, then sat down to read the printed contents of the CD while Kevin worked. The first two pages were the copy of a cover letter detailing a Freedom of Information Act filed against the FBI by a broad coalition of progressive California organizations. The Chicanosaurus Art Collective had been party to the FOIA, with a "cc" sent to Marco Layola. One midnight in July, Synarkist guerrilla cells attacked the Bohemian Grove's meeting with waves of hang gliders and microlites. They bombed the secret get-together with vicious psychochemical drugs and livecast the whole operation. The FBI used the attack as a pretense to conduct mass raids, detentions, and arrests against the wider progressive community. The remaining pages were of the actual FBI documents referencing the Bureau's actions, but they were so heavily redacted Jesse had trouble deciphering them. Somebody had conveniently marked up the originals in five places where the moniker HOOLIGAN-X appeared. From what Jesse could glean from context, HOOLIGAN-X was not an FBI confidential informant but an undercover agent. He was also high up in the leadership of the Bohemian Grove protest and a member of DUI.

"Damn," Kevin said, with twenty-five minutes on the clock. "So, the weird news is that the message on your cell appears to be authentic."

"Meaning what?"

Kevin turned his attention to Jesse.

"The message itself doesn't seem to be composed of different snippets of David speaking, the segments pieced together into some jerry-rigged whole. That's my analysis, backed up by at least three separate tests. First, I looked at the words of the message themselves. Then I cataloged Pickett's previous words from past podcasts and YouTubes and compared them to the words on the message. Finally, I analyzed the background noise on the message itself. In my humble opinion, that message is real. Authentic. Genuine. Every digital test that I can throw at it or run it through proves it. Either that or this is the cleverest, most sophisticated forgery I've ever run across. CIA-level forgery. No. Fucking *Mossad*-level forgery. Which is ridiculous. Why would anybody be interested in counterfeiting a message from David Pickett?"

"Good question."

"Good question, indeed." Kevin cocked an eye. "So, who's this Toby?"

Jesse told Kevin about Tobias in a rush—their acquaintance, seeing him in the park before the riot, witnessing the restaurateur's murder—in a cathartic confession.

"I can't say for certain that Tobias gunned down Spencer's owner," Jesse said. Pleaded. "I need to know what I'm dealing with here."

"Back on fleek." Kevin returned to his screens. "There are only three possibilities here. One: David is still alive. Two: David is somehow communicating with you from beyond the grave. Or three: The message is fake. Our next step is to track the message from your phone to where it was sent. Meaning I start with your smartphone; trace the signal to your local cell tower, down along the wire or fiberoptic line to the wireless access point and the multiport switch where its routed through a T1 or T3 or microwave backhaul; then back out the backhaul on the other end, up through that switch to the far cell tower, and finally out to the origin cellphone. It sounds long and complicated, but actually, it's quite simple and quick. Or potentially so."

He busied himself with keyboard and mouse, then sat back. After fifteen minutes, Kevin frowned and leaned into the screen. His fingers typed furiously. This time, he concentrated on the computer's activities for the next twenty minutes, only to shake his head in disbelief.

"That's impossible," he mumbled.

"What's the matter," Jesse asked.

"The trace. It worked, but not the way it was supposed to. Every hop and stop was correct, and trackable, except that they aren't. I can't resolve where the hell the call came from. The source, the starting device, or the precise route it took. It's a fucking mystery."

"How's that possible?"

"I can't even begin to tell you. I ran the trace twice more. It resolved correctly each time, but it wasn't the same. I can't explain it. It doesn't make any sense. I don't know about you, but I don't believe in the hereafter or that David Pickett is calling you from it. Which means he was either still alive when you got that message, or this is all an elaborate hoax."

"Okay, so what do you want me to do?"

"You only owe me for an hour. I'll keep running traces on this, trying to figure it out. I'm a dog with a bone now."

Jesse gave Kevin his fee via Square. He noticed a pile of Day-Glo cardboard glasses with reflective foil for lenses in a rack next to the door, like old-school 3-D glasses or eclipse shades.

"What's this?" He picked one up.

"Cheap PUD scanners." Kevin continued typing. "I wired 'em to intercept public and private PUD broadcasts and project them onto the lenses. Just press the 'third eye' symbol on the bridge to switch broadcasts."

"Cool!" Jesse grinned. He slipped on a pair and was immediately hovering one hundred fifty meters away, nine meters in the air, observing a traffic accident on Potrero. Pressed the switch and he sailed over Mission residences toward Bernal Heights. If only he'd had a pair when the six young men were gunned down in the BART plaza. "I'll take a couple."

"They're free. I want to give people the power to watch the watchers."

"Thanks for your efforts on the message." Jesse slipped the Fetch back into the knapsack. "Let me know what you find."

"I'll let you know tomorrow morning." Kevin smiled. "Meantime, I got a little surprise for you. Check your email when you get home."

Kevin had spent more than three hours on Jesse's issue. On the trek back to his apartment by way of Cesar Chavez and the homeless tent city along its sidewalks, Jesse did some grocery shopping for staples at People's Picnic. A TV screen above the checkout stand carried a live broadcast of the joint press conference held by the mayor's office and SFPD where the murdered restaurant owner was lavishly mourned; the rioters were mercilessly condemned, the six dead youngsters were dismissed as gangsters committing crimes, and the proper authorities were only mildly excoriated.

Chú Giáp, a cheap Vietnamese restaurant that served excellent phở, was crammed. A hangout for the city's precariat, the establishment had witnessed a pitched ideological battle between David Pickett's DUI and Angie Markham's PU over union raiding that descended into a screaming match between the two. The place had been a favorite of Angie's, who once said their soup was the best cure for a hangover. Jesse stopped his heart from clutching with the memory. He couldn't commit to the relationship out of fear and couldn't tell her out of more fear. He picked up a quart of thin sliced beef and noodle soup to go. Exiting, he noticed Stenny Amps entering, but both avoided acknowledging each other. He was in his living room fifteen minutes later, the groceries put away in his kitchen, his Fetch open and logged on, a second card left by Investigator Van Cornin in his pocket. The smell of cilantro with beefy broth scented the air.

The Internet buzzed with the call from an *ad hoc* coalition of Latinx and progressive community organizations to occupy the Mission tomorrow. The police identified the six Latino men who died as Mara Salvatrucha members and arguments raged over whether they had displayed guns in the inconclusive UAV videos being broadcast by the media. Rumors continued to swirl around government or corporate involvement in David Pickett's death. David remained a riddle wrapped in a mystery inside an enigma. Lively discussions over plans for the Dolores Park rally on social media were quickly superseded by angry debates about the call by a loose network of anarchist, ultra-leftist, and Synarkist groups for concurrent antifascist black bloc actions.

Kevin's email attachment, in MPEG format, was a crude video that Kevin had obviously enhanced. The opening panorama was aerial, shot at night through streamers of smoke and pillars of fire. A crowd ringed a confrontation in progress. Black-clad protesters surrounded an individual dressed in a white chef's smock, brandishing a shotgun, in the middle of a block. There was no sound. The video was granular. A tall lanky Mohawked man, dressed in black, stepped out of the throng and pulled a gun. Four muzzle flashes. The white aproned man fell away.

Jesse identified a figure on the fringe of the crowd. Blurred, stunned, through smoke and flame. He recognized himself.

FOUR

Jesse woke to the Skype chime on his Fetch and the vibration on his smartphone. He rolled out of bed and smacked the start button for his coffee maker before opening his Fetch and beginning the Skype session. Kevin's pixilated image appeared on the screen.

"Tracking a particular cellphone involves three related dimensions." Kevin launched into this discussion before Jesse was completely awake. "Three axes form a mobile tracking field. The x-axis is the provider, which acts as a gateway for the cellphone user's messages and furnishes the IP address, which piggybacks on the mobile phone's MSISDN, or phone number, of the SIM card. The y-axis is the GPS signal from the cellphone when it's turned on. The z-axis is the triangulation of all messages from that cellphone through available network cell towers."

Jesse poured himself a mug of coffee when the percolation reached its peak. He opened the apartment window, then took the Fetch in one hand, the steaming coffee mug in the other hand, and stepped out onto his fire escape. Knots of people moved continuously along the street in the foggy morning light.

"I used one of my most sophisticated trackbots, ran six separate top-of-the-line traces, and got six separate results for each of these mobility factors." Kevin rattled on. "Each time I ran down that one voicemail, I got a different provider and a different cellphone number. Six different providers and six different phone numbers. The cell tower triangulations were similarly mixed. The cellphone broadcasts originated from the corners of Haymarket Street and Pall Mall in

London; Delancey and Suffolk Streets in Manhattan; Rue Daguerre and Gassendi in Paris; Avenida Presidente Mararyk and Hegel in Mexico City; Avenida Paseo and Zapata in Havana; and Guangfu and Meiyuan Roads in Shanghai. The GPS positions were completely bizarre, avoiding densely inhabited locations altogether—the middle of the North Pacific gyre; Mount Tahat in the Sahara Desert; a half mile underwater in the mid-Indian Ocean basin; fifty miles above the earth in the mesosphere over Hudson Bay; the Amazon basin at the borders of Peru, Colombia, and Brazil; and Antarctica's subglacial Lake Vostok."

The small groups of people grew larger, formed crowds, then miniature parades. The people stayed on the sidewalks until they couldn't be contained there, finally spilling into the streets. Everyone moved north.

"The data from the trace, from the six traces, is patently false. Or, more accurately, deliberately forged. Faked or not, the digital information I accessed the first time I ran the voicemail should not have changed. But it did. Five subsequent times. And that should be impossible. Someone, or more probably, something changed that digital history. A bot, or some bit of software, is out there changing, no, camouflaging history every time I attempt to read it."

"But to what end?"

"I haven't the faintest idea. If David's still alive, he's doing his very best to hide it. And if David's dead, someone's going to a fuck of a lot of trouble to disguise it."

Jesse eased back in through the window, into his apartment, balancing the Skype session and an empty coffee mug. He made a decision.

"I've got something to do," Jesse said. "And I'll need your help."

He explained the hack he wanted from Kevin as he completed paying the hacker his due. After ending the Skype session but before turning off the Fetch, he checked a local news broadcast for updates on the Occupy the Mission rally. Police departments and public transportation agencies estimated that more than two million people were likely to attend the event, a guess bolstered by aerial shots of thousands exiting from the 16th and 24th Street BART stations in peaceful, orderly crowds. People were being instructed to tune radios, smartphone apps, TVs, and computers to live transmissions of speeches from the rally once it started.

Jesse dressed in neutral deep blues, avoiding logos and graphics on his shirt, windbreaker, and cap, making sure he had nothing except essential ID and money in his pockets. He jammed a pair of cardboard PUD scanners and his cellphone into his front pockets. Then he climbed down from his apartment and exited his building, joining the throngs sweeping up the street. Drones darted above the throngs as parrots wheeled and squealed further into the overcast sky.

Along the way, Jesse tested Kevin's flimsy PUD scanner. He was momentarily overcome by vertigo with a soaring view over the crowds massing along the street he walked. Once used to his altered perception, he used the "third eye" switch to change PUD broadcasts randomly before refolding the clever device into his front pocket. He stopped for a cup of coffee and a breakfast bagel. He wolfed the bagel down with gulps of java as he walked, thinking about what Kevin had said. Was David alive but trying to mask his whereabouts? Or was he dead and was someone or something setting up a "false flag" operation? In either case the question remained: why? Why was so much effort being expended to fake a deceased David's identity, or why was a still living David in need of such elaborate camouflage? Why the cryptic message, and why had Jesse been targeted to receive the mysterious call? At 18th and Guerrero, it was obvious that every street in every direction was completely filled with people, all of them headed toward Dolores Park. Jesse took a detour to the Mission Street Police Station, where he was confronted by a suspicious pair of cops standing guard.

"State your business," the one with a blond crew-cut demanded.

"I need to speak with Investigator Van Cornin," Jesse said.

"And who are you?"

"He left a card asking for me to call. My name's Jesse Steinfeld."

"Wait right here." The blond cop backed into the station.

Several minutes later, he returned.

"Come in."

"If Van Cornin isn't here, I can come back? I've got a demonstration to go to."

"He's here. You can see him."

Jesse found the police station a tempest of activity, most of it frantic and harassed. After all, the building was entirely surrounded by thousands upon thousands of demonstrators, albeit all of them en route to the rally in Dolores Park. He was ushered past a reception desk to a waiting area, where he sat with the dregs of his coffee. The station's thick walls muted the yelling, chanting, and singing from the crowd. A bank of twenty-four video screens behind the reception desk rippled with airborne image after image—no doubt shot by UAVs—of sidewalks, streets, and the park entirely congested with people. The police officer running the displays kept punching a console and cursing, and a sergeant loomed behind him, his expression dark. A vein in the sergeant's forehead bulged. Here and there, a screen would flip off, then back on, and the picture would be replaced by a video of the police massacre of the six gang members in the BART plaza, or of the black bloc protester killing the restaurateur. The officer would switch off the errant massacre and homicide streams with a curse, then replace them with an appropriate PUD view. But the screens kept changing back. Jesse smirked. Kevin was indeed running the hack.

"Jesse Steinfeld?" A harried man in sharp civilian clothes approached and extended a hand. "Thanks for responding to my request to meet. We're busy today, and a bit jammed. If you don't mind, we'll take this into one of the interview rooms."

The man gestured for Jesse to take the hall ahead of him. The investigator was lean and graying. He held a file folder in one hand and a cellphone in the other. The windows in the interview room faced the waiting area, the reception desk with its wall of videos, and the entrance still under guard. After he settled Jesse into a chair, the investigator took the chair opposite him, across a table.

"Do you know why I asked you to come in today?" Van Cornin asked.

"I take it has something to do with the demonstration against this police station last Sunday evening." Jesse had decided to play it cagey, though not too circumspect.

"This is related. But before I talk about my actual concerns, I'd like to point out that we did notice that you participated in that assault on our station."

Van Cornin pulled out four photographs from his folder and slid them across the table, one at a time. All were of the Sunday evening riot in front of the Mission Street Police Station. The first two showed an indistinct white blob on the far edge of the mob, circled in red. The second two were copies of the first two, blown up, the white blob again circled in red, the resolution lost in pixilated graininess.

"Recognize these? They're shots of you at the riot."

"Damn if I can tell who they are."

"Take it from me, these are photos of you. If need be, we can use some pretty sophisticated computer tools to determine that this was you at Sunday's mob action."

"Okay, I never said I wasn't there. But I was clear across the street, nowhere near the fighting. I attended, but I didn't participate, as you claim. I never shouted anything. I never threw anything. I never even heard any police warning to disperse, or any warning that failure to disperse would result in arrest."

"That's because we were too busy fending off a pretty serious attack on our station by armed and dangerous terrorists. We didn't have time for niceties like warning you all to disperse."

"I was there. You have pictures. I wasn't doing anything illegal. I was observing the action, not taking part in it."

"What about these?" Van Cornin pulled two more glossies from his folder. They showed a barely recognizable Jesse taking in the PUD takedown on Guerrero three days earlier from down the block.

"Where am I doing anything illegal? Or even inappropriate? I'm an innocent bystander!"

The investigator slid the pictures back into a pile, tapped them into alignment, and slid them back into the file.

"There were a dozen clandestine, violent anarchist organizations there the evening of the riot, escalating the street fighting into a full-blown insurrection. We have surveillance and intelligence on several hundred known terrorists who were involved—"

"I already told you, I wasn't involved. I'm not a part of any violent anarchist group, and I certainly wasn't at that demonstration as part of any terrorist attack or militant organization. I was there, sure, but all I did was watch what happened that night."

Van Cornin glared. Jesse refused to be cowed. Their staring match was interrupted when a fellow cop entered and whispered in the investigator's ear. Through the interview room windows, Jesse glimpsed the frenetic pace of the police in the rest of the station. Massacre and homicide videos now dominated the screens behind the reception desk.

"I'll get back to your role in the riot. Now, let's talk about what you did after the assault on the police station. After that mob of yours rampaged up and down Valencia, laying waste to everything on the street. After you and your crew killed Sam Barbier, the Spencer's Restaurant owner."

"What the fuck do you mean, my mob, my crew? I didn't riot. I didn't kill anybody."

"The video's been all over the media. Showing the whole damned murder. In digital detail."

"Do you mean *that* video?" Jesse jammed a finger at the twenty-four videos at the reception desk. A quarter of them showed the Valencia Street homicide. And not the abbreviated video shown by the media, but the full version that Kevin had sent him. "Go ahead, bring in a screen if you want. Magnify the video to your heart's content. You know damn well what it will show. That I ran up to that confrontation in front of that restaurant when it was in progress, when that fucker stepped out and blasted the restaurant owner. There was nothing premeditated about that, not on my part. That fucking video proves it."

"I find it difficult to accept that you were around for the assault on the UAV and in the crowd during the riot and then wound up in front of that Valencia restaurant when the homicide occurred—and it was all a coincidence. I don't believe in coincidence. If I were writing fiction, all these 'coincidences' would come off as extremely contrived."

"Look, I did nothing wrong. And nothing illegal. If you want to charge me with a crime, do so. If not, I'm getting fed up with this so-called interview. I've got a demonstration to go to."

"You're telling me you don't have any connection with Tobias Barnabas?"

The investigator stopped for effect. They waited each other out in silence. The wall of videos was settling back to covering the demonstration outside.

"Is Toby Barnabas wanted?" Jesse finally asked, cautiously.

"We haven't charged this Tobias Barnabas with anything," Van Cornin said, now equally cautious. "Let alone with the shooting of Spencer restaurateur Samuel Barbier. However, we consider him a person of interest in the homicide of Barbier and would like to talk to him. Unfortunately, he seems to have gone to ground."

"Off the record," Jesse said, after a pause. "I know Toby Barnabas only in passing. He's not a friend, and barely an acquaintance. For the record, the man in the video may or may not be Toby Barnabas, but I don't know who shot the restaurant owner on Valencia last Sunday."

The pause was even longer this time.

"We'd be grateful for your help," Van Cornin finally said. "Any help you could give us, in catching whoever murdered Sam Barbier."

Jesse left the police station and walked into streets crammed with now hushed demonstrators. Someone had managed to scrawl *He Lives!* in dripping red spray-paint on the station's facade. He noticed Ari

Moser across the jammed space, and they exchanged salutes. No one moved, and a glimpse through the PUD scanner revealed that Dolores Park was packed solid with demonstrators who spilled into the surrounding neighborhoods in every direction, occupying everything for blocks around. The rally had started. Speeches echoed from nearby cellphones and the far-off park.

"They are gunning down our young men in the streets. ¡Como perros!"

There was no mass movement possible, but people could still move individually as long as they did so carefully. He eased his way gradually up 18th toward the park, beneath spirals of parakeets in flight, using the PUD scanner to scope out his surroundings from drone height. It appeared that the antifascist black bloc, tens of thousands strong and growing, had positioned itself on the northern edge of the massive demonstration, occupying the streets from 16th to the old Armory.

"¡Basta! It's time to say 'enough!' No more!"

Additional police cars raced from the surrounding city to join the cops who'd taken up a northern perimeter around the black bloc, sirens wailing, anticipating what was to come. "They say there are four million of us at this demonstration," a woman with earbuds marveled next to him, "occupying these streets." The antifascists, now numbering in the hundreds of thousands, had decided not to wait. Jesse reached the intersection of 18th and Dolores and noticed a tall female Goth, her leather jacket emblazoned with a "Tank Girl" graphic, walking casually up Dolores beneath cawing ravens and strings of papel picado. Cynthia.

"The police and FBI are stormtroopers for state and capital. ¡Ellos son asesinos!"

Figures all in black rushed the police lines, thousands of them, wave after wave overrunning the police cars, overturning them, setting them ablaze, ignoring the paltry clouds of tear-gas wafting around the battle. Dancers plumed in ostrich-feather headdresses paraded by. He followed Cynthia at a cautious distance. She would stop, look around surreptitiously, then start walking again when she gauged the coast was clear. He kept tailing Cynthia, ignoring Angie Markham across the street as she gesticulated plaintively with one hand while holding up one corner of her *An Injury to One Is an Injury to All* banner with the other hand.

"¿Quién se beneficia? Comrade Pickett's murder is political, but so are the murders of our young *hombres*."

Jesse played coy following Cynthia, who pretended to wander even as she kept to an obvious direction. She dissembled once again at the corner of 19th, feigning interest in a peddler's handmade beaded jewelry and *cempasúchil* bouquets. Not-so-distant explosions accompanied columns of smoke and flame racing into the sky amid fleeing flocks of frightened parrots. Glimpses through the PUD scanner showed the rioting black bloc now rampaging up the 101 off-ramp and on-ramp. Storming heaven.

"To our *compañeros de correrías* in the *Bloque Negro*, we salute your bravery even as we disagree with your tactics and politics. *¡Tu lucha es nuestra lucha!*"

The antifascists quickly overran the eastern freeway, surging toward the intersection with 101 running north and south. Trapped cars honked ineffectually. "The governor has just declared martial law," someone nearby said while listening to a smartphone. "The National Guard is mobilizing from Treasure Island." Children waved copal incense sticks as they passed. Cynthia glanced stealthily around, then ducked into a bank of hedges.

"*¡Solidaridad con el pueblo Mexicano!* These are not just our streets, this our land. Without our land, there can be no freedom. *¡Es mejor morir de pie que vivir de rodillas!*"

Olive-green motorcycles, jeeps, armored personnel vehicles, anti-riot trucks, and tanks full of troops wearing urban camouflage rumbled across the Bay Bridge and down 101 toward a confrontation with the expanding riot. Crows gathered on wing for the battle. Cynthia hugged a smirking Toby amid the shrubbery. Jesse's smartphone rang with the incessant guitar thrum of Leonard Cohen's "Partisan." When had he turned the ringer back on? He answered. "Jesse, this is David Pickett."

SAN FRANCISCO MISSION MAP

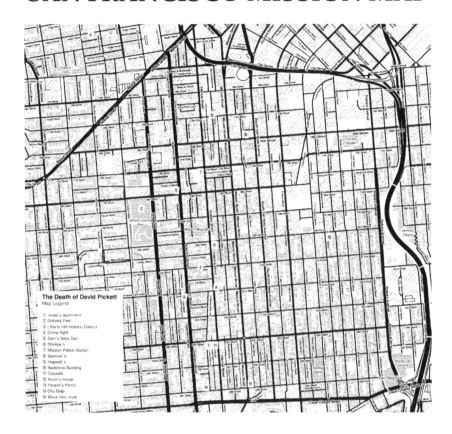

The Death of David Pickett
Map Legend

1: Jesse's apartment
2: Dolores Park
3: Liberty Hill Historic District
4: Drone fight
5: Sam's Sons Deli
6: Stumpy's
7: Mission Police Station
8: Spencer's
9: Hopwell's
10: Redstone Building
11: Goyaałé
12: Kevin's house
13: People's Picnic
14: Chu Giáp
15: Black bloc zone

ACKNOWLEDGEMENTS

Many individuals helped me to produce this book, starting with Scott Mullen who provided the valuable initial read through. Amelia Beamer supplied developmental and line editing, and Bob Cooper did the copy editing of the manuscript. Jon Hunt produced the cover art and illustrations as well as various design elements.

Behind this effort, from start to finish, has been my wife, Kay Taneyhill. Without Kay's love, encouragement, and support, my writing and this book would not have been possible.

ILLUSTRATIONS

Jon Hunt produced the cover art and illustrations for *Dusted by Stars*. He also did the covers for my two previous books (*1% Free* and *The Death of David Pickett*), the black & white illustration of Becky Wiley, and various design elements (my company logo and the galaxy dingbat). When I find a graphic artist/illustrator whose work I like I stick with them. He can be reached at www.huntillustration.com.

That said, there is one illustration in this book that wasn't done by Jon, the grayscale graphic of Commune al-Mirrīkh on page 23. Originally a color PNG by Kevin Gill called A Living Mars: A Visualization of Mars, Very Much Alive, he described the process of creating the illustration as follows: "A visualization of an Earth-like Mars, be it ancient or a future of terraforming. This was produced by rendering a flat model image using the MRO MOLA 128 pix/deg elevation dataset in jDem846 then layering imagery from Blue Marble in GIMP. The layer was then brought back into jDem to produce the final spherical projection and scripted to add the atmosphere and clouds from the NASA Visible Earth catalog. Eye position is about 6,600 kilometers (4100 miles) from the surface of the planet and looking at the southern hemisphere (~20° South) and the 180th meridian."

I converted Gill's PNG to a PDF using Preview on my Mac, applied a grayscale Quartz filter, sharpened the image, and converted it into a JPEG. Then I added the two captions and four scenic bubbles of quasi-alien landscapes to create a tourist infographic memorializing a future socialist Mars.

There are also two maps. The San Francisco Mission District map for *The Death of David Pickett* was generated using the toner filter applied to Open Street Map data using Stamen Design cartography tools (maps.stamen.com). I then added the map legend. The Milky Way Galaxy map with overlay diagram was copied from Bruce MacEvoy's Astro index page "Overview of the Galaxy" (www.handprint.com/ASTRO/galaxy.html). I grayscaled it, then added two notes identifying locations of importance in *Dusted by Stars*. I have never been able to write without making maps.

ABOUT THE AUTHOR

G.A. Matiasz was born in 1952. A late hippie and an early punk, he began self-publishing at 17 with a high school underground newpaper, and burned his draft card at age 18. Essays from his publication *Point-Blank/San Diego's Daily Impulse* have been reprinted in *Semiotext[e] USA*, the *Utne Reader*, and War Resisters' League's short-lived youth publication *SPEW!* He has also published essays in *Against The Wall*, the *New Indicator*, *Draft NOtices*, and the *San Diego Newsline*. His first science fiction novel *End Time: Notes on the Apocalypse* was published in 1994 by AK Press and was reprinted in Portuguese by a Brazilian publisher, Conrad Livros. G.A. Matiasz lives in San Francisco, where he wrote a monthly column of news analysis and political commentary for *Maximum Rocknroll* under the name "Lefty" Hooligan from 1992 to 2020. The 2018 speculative mystery *The Death of David Pickett* is a prequel to his 2016 near-future science fiction thriller *1% Free*, which are published by 62 Mile Press. *Dusted by Stars* is a space opera set in the same fictional universe *circa* 2390.

BOOKS BY THE AUTHOR

Fiction by G.A. Matiasz:
End Time: Notes on the Apocalypse
1% Free
The Death of David Pickett
Dusted by Stars

More information on 62 Mile Press: www.62milepress.com

Made in the USA
Las Vegas, NV
24 February 2022